Love is
a time of enchantment:
in it all days are fair and all fields
green. Youth is blest by it,
old age made benign: the eyes of love see
roses blooming in December,
and sunshine through rain. Verily
is the time of true-love
a time of enchantment — and
Oh! how eager is woman
to be bewitched!

THE FIRST OFFICER

Katy and Charles, separated for four years
met again aboard a luxurious yacht, she
the guest of a Greek millionaire, he the
First Officer. From that moment, Katy
realised that she still loved Charles,
and also that it was her fault that
their marriage failed. Charles had been
disillusioned with her once – could
she get him to change his mind? Or
should she take the chance to start a
new life without him?

ANNE WEALE

THE FIRST
OFFICER

Complete and Unabridged

ULVERSCROFT
Leicester

A-1

First published in Great Britain in 1980 by
Mills & Boon Limited
London

First Large Print Edition
published July 1991
by arrangement with
Mills & Boon Limited
London

British Library CIP Data

Weale, Anne *1929* –
The first officer. — Large print ed. —
Ulverscroft large print series: romance
I. Title
823.914

ISBN 0–7089–2472–7

Published by
F. A. Thorpe (Publishing) Ltd.
Anstey, Leicestershire
Set by Words & Graphics Ltd.
Anstey, Leicestershire
Printed and bound in Great Britain by
T. J. Press (Padstow) Ltd., Padstow, Cornwall

1 ✕

KATY was getting ready for her dinner date with Robert Otterway. She had brushed her thick ash-brown hair and piled it on top of her head, secured by three diamanté combs. She had stroked the lids of her eyes with green, gold and brown shadow-sticks to emphasise the colours in her irises, and brushed her long, curling lashes with dark brown mascara. As she was painting her mouth, there was a tap on the door and Thalia strolled into the bedroom, a drink in one hand, a cigarette in the other.

Katy's colouring was subtle. Thalia's was much more dramatic; black curly hair cropped close in what she called her Greek goatherd's style, a make-up like a pale mask, and sapphire blue eyes which had a very slight cast, more noticeable when she was tired, which gave her a striking resemblance to a Siamese cat.

Thalia Harcourt had started life as one of six children of a London bus driver, living in a small terraced villa in the outermost suburbs. Now, approaching her thirtieth birthday, she occupied a penthouse flat in one of the most fashionable districts of central London where she had three boutiques, and where clothes designed by her were to be seen in the smartest hotels and restaurants and, when their first owners had done with them, were re-sold by dress agencies to women who could not afford to buy them new.

Katy, who was five years younger than Thalia, had also undergone a considerable change of fortune in her lifetime. Her childhood and girlhood had been cushioned by luxury and then, for a time, she had come down in the world, and suffered considerable hardship until she had learned how to live for a month on what her extravagant father would have spent on a single lavish meal.

Now, living in Thalia's apartment, and employed by the famous designer to oil the wheels of her private life, Katy had regained many of the comforts of her earlier years. But the time in between had changed her from what she could recognise now as a spoilt, wilful, self-centred girl into a quite different and, she hoped, much more likeable person.

Sometimes, remembering what she had been like before a long spell of misfortune had knocked all the nonsense out of her, she felt hot and cold with shame for her past stupidities.

Everything Charles had said of her during that last furious row — all the harsh indictments which at the time she had denied, thinking him the one at fault — had been true.

She had wanted the kind of man he was — tough, adventurous, virile, masterful — but she had not been ready to pay the price for being that kind of man's woman; had not even realised, then, that there was any price to be paid.

Now she knew better, but now it was four years too late. She was in London, living under an assumed name, and Charles might be anywhere in the Seven Seas. The likelihood of their ever meeting again was as slight as the chance which had brought them together in the first place when, sailing his sloop round a headland at sunrise on a summer morning, he had seen her standing on the private beach below her father's ill-gotten villa, shedding her nightdress before walking, naked, into the sea for her pre-breakfast bathe.

Five minutes earlier she would have been in her bedroom. Five minutes later the sloop would have passed out of sight beyond the other promontory which sheltered the bay and kept the water there calm and transparent even when a fresh breeze was blowing over the sea.

"Where is Robert taking you this evening?" Thalia asked, coming to sit in the chair alongside Katy's dressing-table.

Katy told her. Having finished making up her face, she rose from the stool and went to take her dress from the wardrobe. Had she wished, she could have bought clothes designed by Thalia for very much less than their retail price, but she never did so, preferring to shop at chain stores and to invest most of her salary. Long ago, as a rich man's daughter, she had worn clothes even more expensive than those bearing Thalia's label, but now it seemed more important to safeguard herself against the possibility of a third disaster befalling her. Not that her post as Thalia's housekeeper was insecure.

The designer liked men, and had been involved in a love affair ever since Katy had known her. But it was not the kind of relationship which ended in marriage. Indeed Thalia said frankly that there was no point in her marrying. She had no desire to have children, was more than capable of supporting herself. She needed a man only as a partner in bed, a rôle which, according to her, no one could sustain successfully for more than a year or two. In fact her current affair had lasted since shortly before Katy had begun to work for her, two years ago; but now it was on the wane and, although he might not realise it, Philip was going to be dropped as soon as someone else caught Thalia's fancy.

"It's a good thing everyone doesn't have your flair for changing the belt on a little number from Oxford Street and making it look like that," said Thalia, when Katy was dressed. "It's largely your figure, of course."

She herself was too thin for beauty, if not for elegance. But Katy was blessed with slim legs and a narrow waist with curves above and below it.

They chatted about this and that until

the sound of the doorbell heralded the arrival of Robert, whom Katy had met at a party two months before. He was the first man she had dated on more than the most casual basis in all the long years since the débâcle with Charles from which she had barely recovered before her father's arrest had come as another shattering blow.

"Ask him in for a drink, if there's time," Thalia suggested.

Although very different in temperament, she and Katy were now close friends as well as employer and employee. They had met in the days when Katy was one of a team of girls working for a woman who organised private dinner parties for hostesses who wanted and could afford to have everything done for them. On that occasion the party had been given by a woman TV presenter. While Katy was loading the dishwasher after the meal, Thalia had come into the kitchen and chatted to her. A few days later she had telephoned the catering firm and booked Katy for a similar party at her penthouse. The upshot of their second encounter had been an invitation to Katy to come to work for her full-time.

"What I need, in effect," Thalia had explained, "is someone to take all the household problems off my shoulders and leave me free to concentrate on my work in the way a successful man can. You see, the reason that I'm not married is because I prefer to live life entirely *my* way, and marriage — if it's going to work — is a matter of continual compromise."

"I see. But — I must admit — I was wondering if, being a designer, you might be a rather difficult, moody person to work for," Katy had told her frankly.

Thalia had laughed. "First and foremost I'm a businesswoman, and that calls for plenty of self-discipline, physical and mental. No moods. No fits of temperament."

So, after thinking it over, Katy had accepted the job and had moved from a rather drab bedsitter into much more comfortable quarters which included a small sitting-room of her own and, adjoining her blue and white bedroom, a bathroom as luxurious as those to which she had been used in her earlier life.

When she opened the door to Robert Otterway, he was carrying a bunch of pink

7

rosebuds protected from the winter night air by transparent wrappings.

"Oh, Robert, for me? How lovely!" she exclaimed, as he handed them to her. "Come in and let me introduce you to Thalia. She's having a quiet evening at home."

Having ushered him into the huge, lofty-ceilinged room which combined the functions of sitting-room, dining-room and workroom, and presented him to the other woman, she left them exchanging pleasantries while she went to the kitchen to put the roses in water.

It was the first time he had brought her flowers and, as it was not her birthday, she could only conclude that he had something to celebrate, or that tonight he planned to advance their relationship on to a new plane.

Throughout their first four or five dates she had been prepared for him to make a pass at her, and had been both relieved and puzzled when he had not even kissed her. They both moved in circles where premarital and extra-marital love affairs were the norm, and since meeting Robert and growing quite fond of him, Katy had begun to think there was little point in continuing to abstain from the carefree, impermanent relationships which were going on all round her.

After the break-up with Charles, and following her father's trial and imprisonment for bribery, and his subsequent death from a heart attack, there had been a long period of time when she had been too numbed by disillusionment and grief to be capable of any emotion. This had been followed by a phase when she had lived with the hope that Charles might somehow come back into her life. Now she had accepted the fact that he never would, and that the longing for love which he had aroused in her would have to be satisfied by someone else.

She returned to the living-room to find Thalia and Robert seated a yard apart on one of the curving white sofas which formed one of the room's several sitting areas. Thalia was being charming and amusing, and Robert was responding, but Katy had a feeling that this was merely urbanity, and they did not take to each other.

Her impression was confirmed later on when, on their way to the theatre in his car, Robert said, "Rather a frightening female, your boss."

"Frightening? Thalia? Oh, no, not a bit. She's a darling."

"I'll take your word for it, but she's certainly not my kind of darling — too brittle, too sure of herself. I prefer a much softer kind of woman." He removed one hand from the steering wheel to place it over her smaller hands, clasped in her lap, and give them a gentle squeeze. "Like you," he added.

As he put his hand back on the wheel, Katy had a sudden mental vision of another man's hand; a hand as different from Robert's as her looks were different from Thalia's. Robert's hand was the soft, pale hand of a man who worked in an office in a northern climate. The hand which filled her mind's eye was the strong, sunburned hand of a man whose profession was seamanship.

After the play, he took her to dine in Soho. They began with hot grapefruit with rum, followed by chicken Kiev which the waiter had pierced before serving so that the melted butter sealed within the crisply-coated chicken breasts should not spurt out and spoil Katy's dress.

Towards the end of their meal Robert said, "It's rather noisy in here tonight. Shall we have our coffee at my place?"

It was the approach she had known must come sooner or later and which, when it did, she had made up her mind to accept.

"Yes, why not?" she agreed. "I should like to see where you live, Robert."

"It's neither as large nor as lavish as where you live," he warned her. "But it suits me for the time being."

While he checked the bill she watched his face, and wondered how many women there had been before her in his life. He was a good-looking man with brown hair and friendly blue eyes, but he did not cause women to stare as they had when Charles Ormond passed.

Charles had possessed something rare among men in the modern world; an air of wildness, not in the pejorative sense, but in the sense of being free from the ties which kept most men and women in lifelong bondage. Anyone watching him striding along a Mediterranean waterfront would have seen at a glance that here was no holidaying businessman; that such magnificent fitness was never achieved by jogging round a city park or spending an hour on a squash court after a day at the office.

The lean and hard-muscled grace of Charles' tall frame had been as beautiful to watch as the fluid movements of a panther and, in a way, he had lived rather like a panther, eating only when he was hungry, walking for miles whenever he was ashore, and never abusing his body as most people did by smoking or spending his evenings slumped in a chair watching television. Watching the box would have bored him, as did all spectator sports. Charles was a doer, and a loner; a man who had only to see a difficult rock face to want to climb it, or a wide bay to want to swim it, or a beautiful girl to want to make love to her.

Why am I thinking of him now, of all times? Katy wondered, as they walked to where Robert had parked his car.

She supposed it must be because, if she let Robert take her to bed, it would be the first time she had surrendered herself since the last time Charles had made love to her, four empty years ago. Several men had kissed her since then, but none had stirred her as the memory of Charles's lovemaking could stir her; nor, indeed, did Robert excite her. But she was as much drawn to him as she was ever likely to be drawn to anyone, and she could not go on living on memories indefinitely. The ghost of Charles, which had held her in thrall for so long, had to be exorcised, and the most effective way to do it seemed to be to embark on a new relationship with a flesh and blood man.

Nevertheless, as Robert drove down the ramp to a basement garage beneath a large block of flats, she almost changed her mind and asked him to take her home; not from nervousness, but from an irrational sense of guilt, as if she were on the brink of an act of betrayal. Then she told herself firmly that it was absurd to feel conscience-stricken about a man from whom she had parted four years ago, and who undoubtedly had made love to any number of women since then.

In the lift, Robert pressed the button for the second floor, and very soon they were stepping into the corridor leading to his front door. He worked for a merchant bank and although, as he had said, his flat was not as spacious or spectacular as Thalia's much-photographed penthouse, he lived in the style of a man with a very comfortable income and the taste of his parents' class. Katy knew, from the mutual friend who had introduced them, that his father was a retired General who lived in a manor house in Suffolk, and his mother was the President of the village Women's Institute and spent her time gardening and embroidering kneelers for the parish church.

Katy herself was the child of a self-made man who had lived in the flashy style of the newly rich until her expensive education at an English boarding school and a Swiss finishing school had enabled her to restrain his taste for all the most vulgar forms of opulence. She could scarcely remember her mother who had died when she was six years old but who, by all accounts, had been a down-to-earth Yorkshire girl who might, had she lived, have prevented her husband's disgrace and her daughter's over-indulged upbringing.

Having helped her to take off the fun

14

fur jacket which Thalia had given her the previous Christmas — all the furs and jewels given to her by her father she had sold to pay for her Cordon Bleu cookery training — Robert crossed the room to put a record on the music deck.

She expected him to choose something soft and romantic, and was surprised when she recognised the opening bars of a Brahms symphony which was also one of her favourites, but which seemed an odd choice of background music for what he had in mind.

While he was in the kitchen, making the coffee, she wandered about the sitting-room, looking at his books and pictures. Would he take her home afterwards, or would he expect her to stay the night with him?

She wished he would forget about the coffee, and come back and take her in his arms, instead of leaving her on her own, a prey to renewed guilt feelings.

At last he returned with the tray which he placed on a low glass table in front of the sofa. Then he went to a cupboard for two glasses and a bottle of cognac which he added to the things on the tray.

Smiling, he beckoned her to him. "Come and sit down."

Shivering slightly, Katy walked to the sofa, and he took her hand and drew her down on to the feather-filled cushions. He had kissed her on several occasions, but never very passionately. Now he folded her in his arms and gave her a long, ardent kiss to which she submitted rather than responded.

When he raised his head, he said softly, "I expect you've guessed why I asked you here?"

She felt a spasm of irritation, and was tempted to say, "Don't talk about it, man. Get on with it!"

"I suppose a lot of proposals have been made over restaurant tables, but I prefer rather more privacy when I'm asking a girl to marry me," Robert went on. "Not that I've ever done it before. My parents are beginning to despair that I'll ever find someone to suit me. I haven't told them about you yet. If you say yes, darling, we'll go to see them this weekend. You are going to say yes, aren't you, my sweet, lovely Katy?"

She gazed at him, utterly dumbfounded.

It had never even crossed her mind that he might be seriously in love with her. She had thought him bent on a liaison, and even now could not be certain that she had not misunderstood him.

"You want me to *marry* you, Robert?" she asked, in a tone of bewilderment.

"What else?" he said, smiling down at her. "Surely you must have guessed that I've been in love with you since the second time we met? Women are supposed to have an instinct about these things."

"I thought . . . I thought you wanted to sleep with me," she told him.

"I do — very much. And when I've put this on your finger, and we've drunk a toast to our future together, my next suggestion will be that we adjourn to my bedroom." As he spoke, he took from his pocket a ring-box.

To open it, he had to remove his other arm from around her and, as he did so, she sprang to her feet, exclaiming, "Oh, Robert, this is dreadful! I had no idea . . . *no* idea that you were serious about me. If I had, I should have stopped seeing you."

"Why? You like me . . . I thought you

loved me," he said, beginning to look troubled.

"Yes, I do like you — very much. But you see . . . I'm married already. At least I was married, once. And although it broke up years ago, my husband and I aren't divorced."

"Oh, God! Why didn't you tell me?" he asked, with a groan in his voice.

"It didn't seem important. I didn't dream you were serious about me."

He looked at her long and thoughtfully. "Very serious, my dear," he said, at length. "And I took you for the kind of woman who would only want a serious relationship with a man. I still think I'm right about that. Why did you let me bring you here if you thought I had something else in mind? You're not one of these girls who'll jump into bed in return for an evening out."

"No, I'm not," she agreed. "But we've known each other for some time, and I've grown very fond of you, Robert, and . . . well, I'm tired of being lonely. I have Thalia's friendship, and other friends, but it's not the same as having a man in one's life."

"I see." His eyebrows drawn into a

frown, he bent to pour out the coffee and fill the crystal liqueur glasses.

"You say your marriage ended years ago. It can't have been many years ago, if you're only twenty-four now."

Katy sank into one of the chairs on the opposite side of the table. "We split up four years ago. We'd spent six months together, and then I went back to my father and it was about another six months before the break became final."

"So you were nineteen when you married? That's very young to know one's own mind. How old was your husband?"

"He was twenty-five. He'll be the same age as you now. Thank you" — this as he placed a cup of coffee and a glass on the lamp table between the two armchairs.

Robert drank his cognac in one swallow, and refilled his glass. It was plain that he had had a great shock, as had she, although in a different and less distressing way. To find that a man was in love with you was not as upsetting as the discovery that the woman you loved was not free.

"Why aren't you divorced?" he asked her.

"Charles said he would never divorce me."

As clearly as if it were yesterday, she remembered the biting tone of voice with which her husband had dismissed her father's insistence that the marriage must be dissolved legally as well as effectively. How cold Charles's grey eyes had been: those strange eyes, the colour of silver, made all the more striking by the dark bronze-brown of his sun-tanned, wind-whipped yachtsman's skin.

She went on, "He said there could be no question of his ever marrying again, and it would be a public service to prevent me from making myself as bad a wife to someone else as I had been to him. He was very angry when he said it, and perhaps he feels differently now, but I have no idea where he is. Anyway, until now, no one else has wanted to marry me."

Robert seated himself on the edge of the sofa, opposite her, his hands clasped between his spread knees, his expression a blend of anxiety and determination.

"I'm quite sure that, with me, you would be everything a man could desire in a wife. I don't know much about the current divorce laws, except that they've been greatly eased in recent years. It may be that you can get your freedom quite easily, on the grounds of desertion. I'll find out about that tomorrow. If it's necessary to get his agreement to an official separation, then I'm sure he could be traced without too much difficulty. What did he do for his living?"

"He'd been in the Navy for a time, and then he'd resigned his commission to sail his own boat round the world. When I met him, he was knocking about the Mediterranean, living on a legacy from his grand mother."

"Hmph, he doesn't sound the sort of chap I should want my nineteen-year-old daughter to marry. I'm surprised your father allowed it."

"He didn't approve, but he couldn't stop me. I was over age."

"So this man married you against your father's wishes? Not a very straight way to behave," Robert said disapprovingly.

"Charles never liked my father. I think he suspected the truth. I'm afraid I have something even more unpleasant to tell you, Robert." She took a small sip of the brandy. "Brown is not my real surname. My married name was . . . is Ormond. After Charles left, I reverted to my maiden name, which was White. I'm the daughter of Howard White who, three years ago, was sent to prison for bribing local government officials and for offences against the foreign exchange control laws. Perhaps you remember his trial — it was the scandal of the year. So you see, apart from being married, I'm not at all the kind of person your parents would find acceptable as a daughter-in-law."

"Good God!" he exclaimed, staring at her in stupefaction. "Yes, of course I remember the trial. But he was a terrible man — not only a crook, but a boor, the very worst sort of rough diamond. I can't believe you're his daughter."

He saw the pain in her eyes. "Oh, my dear girl, I'm sorry — I shouldn't have said that. I'm just so staggered by all this. You've never talked much about yourself, but I always assumed your background was similar to mine, or would have been, had your parents still been alive."

"No, my manner is just a veneer acquired at boarding school. Under the

22

surface, I'm as different from you as chalk from cheese. My father was born in a back street in Birmingham, and my mother's family were farm workers. I'm not the wife for you, Robert, even if I didn't have one failed marriage behind me."

She rose from the chair and went to join him on the sofa. She had known too much anguish herself to want to inflict any hurt on someone as nice as Robert Otterway. Moved by an urge to comfort him for the unintentional shocks she had inflicted on him, she put both hands on his forearm and said gently, "But if you would like me to be your girl-friend for a while, I think we could give each other a good deal of happiness."

He turned and took her in his arms, not to kiss her, but to hold her against him, his face buried in her soft hair.

"No, no, I don't want that," he murmured. "I want you — but as my wife. I don't care whose daughter you are. You're gentle and kind and very beautiful, and I'm sure my people will adore you when they get to know you as I do. But they're fairly old-fashioned in some ways, so it would be better to get your freedom organised before announcing our engagement."

He tilted her head and kissed her lightly on the lips.

"I'm going to take you home now. Had we been engaged . . . but I hope we shall be, very soon. Until then — " He put her away from him.

Katy watched him going to fetch her jacket and, instead of being gratified by his chivalry, she felt a tinge of impatience. Charles would have been less high-minded. Charles, knowing she was a virgin, because he had asked her, had no compunction about making love to her, not only before they were married, but before he had told her he loved her.

With a sudden sharp thrust of excitement in the pit of her stomach, she remembered the hot afternoon when they had sailed to a bay where no one else ever went, and where, on cushions on the foredeck, under a sky the colour of cornflowers, he had removed her bikini and made long, delectable love to her. Only afterwards had he said, "I think you're the girl for me, Katy. Do you fancy a sea-roving life? Would you like to marry me?"

And she, not knowing what was involved,

24

and unused to the slightest hardship, had blithely said, "Yes . . . oh, *yes*, Charles!"

The living-room was still alight and Thalia was busy at her drawing-board when Katy opened the door.

"Hi. Good time?" Thalia enquired, leaning back in her chair and rubbing the back of her neck.

"Yes, the play was good and so was our meal. Have you been working all evening? Would you like a cup of hot choc?"

"Yes, and a snack of some sort. The supper you left was delicious, but that was three hours ago."

The designer could eat and drink all the fattening things which most women had to deny themselves without putting on an ounce.

Katy went into the kitchen and made an open sandwich and chocolate for Thalia, and a mug of hot Bovril for herself. When she returned to the big room Thalia had left her working area and was putting on a tape which proved to be Diana Ross's 'Touch Me In The Morning' recording.

She turned down the volume control so that the music made an agreeable background sound, and came to where Katy had put the tray on a brass and glass table.

"I don't think your boy-friend approved of me."

"Or you of him," said Katy, a shade dryly. "He's asked me to marry him," she added.

"Oh, Katy, no — he's not for you. You haven't accepted him, have you?"

"No."

"Good." Thalia sounded relieved. "And I'm not just saying that for the selfish reason that I don't want to lose you."

"You only had a short chat with him. How can you tell what he's like, or that he and I shouldn't suit each other?"

"I may not know much about him, but I think I know you pretty well. You need the kind of man who will be as exacting and satisfying as my career is to me. Robert Otterway isn't like that. He's comfortable, safe and, after a time, pretty dull. You would run his home to perfection, be an ideal mum, and, at forty, be bored out of your mind."

"I think it sounds a nice life. But I couldn't have it if I wanted it. I had to tell him about my father, and although Robert says it's not important, I'm sure when he's thought it over he'll realise that it does matter."

Thalia knew about Howard White, but she didn't know about Charles. There had been times when Katy had been tempted to confide in her, but always she had held back.

"If he does come to that conclusion, it will prove he's not the right man for you. What the hell has your no good father got to do with you?"

"You may think heredity unimportant, but not everyone does," answered Katy. "Robert's parents are rather old-fashioned, conservative gentlefolk. A man like my father would have given them the shudders."

"Yes, I see that if he were alive he could be an embarrassment to them. But he's not, so why must they know? I think you were foolish to tell Robert, and he will be even more foolish if he tells them. Let the dead past bury its dead, as some poet said."

"I couldn't marry him under a false name."

"No, but White is such a common name that there's no reason why he should have connected you with your father. If they were to trace all their forebears, I should think most people, including the Otterways, would find they had several bad types among their ancestors. However, the deed is done now, and can't be undone, and if it does put him off you, he isn't much of a man."

Katy said nothing to this. She had often wondered what had been Charles's reaction on reading the reports of her father's trial. She had married him knowing little about his family, except that he could not remember his parents and had been brought up by grandparents. But, looking back on their short, stormy life together, she had formed the impression that his background must have been much the same as Robert's.

Charles had never shown his contempt for her father; not even during the one-sided row about their marriage when Howard White had lost his temper and told Charles he would not allow his daughter to throw herself away on a no-good layabout who couldn't begin to keep her in the style to which she was accustomed, and who could forget any ideas he might have of living in luxury at his father-in-law's expense.

"I'm sorry you feel like that, but Katy thinks she can adjust to my standard of living, and I shouldn't dream of allowing you to subsidise us, even if you wanted to do so," Charles had replied with cool courtesy.

"What a strange expression on your face! What are you thinking? Are you angry with me for criticising Robert?" asked Thalia.

"No, no — I was miles away," said Katy, hastily closing her mind to that sudden vision of the terrace of the Spanish villa which, in those days, had been one of Howard White's two holiday homes.

Soon afterwards she went to bed, not to sleep, but to lie awake pondering Robert's proposal of marriage. Even if he were not put off her by finding she was the daughter of a convicted criminal, did she really want to marry him?

Early the following morning, before she had taken in Thalia's breakfast tray, he rang up.

"Did you sleep well? I didn't. I've been awake most of the night, thinking about you, and wanting to make it up to you for all the misery you've been through, my poor love."

This didn't sound as if he were beginning to have second thoughts.

Before she could reply, Robert went on, "Listen, last night you told me that Ormond had been round the world on a boat, and was cruising in the Mediterranean when you met. What was the name of the boat, and her port of registry?"

Katy told him. "Why do you ask that?"

"Because I have a chum who's an underwriter. He can look her up in Lloyd's register of yachts, and perhaps trace her present whereabouts. Are you busy this evening?"

"No, Thalia's dining out, so I'm free."

"How about coming here again, and giving me a sample of your home cooking?"

"With pleasure. What would you like to eat?"

"I'll leave that to you. I'll pick you up at six-thirty. Okay?"

"Okay."

"Till then." He made a kissing noise and rang off.

Katy finished preparing Thalia's breakfast.

She was pouring freshly-ground coffee from the percolator into a warmed white porcelain pot when she heard the click of the letter-box as the hall porter pushed the morning mail through the door.

There were only two letters that morning, both for Thalia. Katy had no one to write to her. She had never had any contact with her relations on either side of the family, and the friendships she had made at school had not been the kind to survive her father's disgrace. Since then she had made some new friends, but when they wanted to contact her they rang up.

She had taken in Thalia's tray, and returned to the kitchen to drink her own tall glass of orange juice and consider what to cook for Robert, when Thalia rang for her.

The designer's bedroom was almost as large as the living-room, and decorated entirely in white. The dominating feature was the huge giltwood four-poster draped with yards of airy white voile.

Thalia, who had bitten off a mouthful of toast and black cherry jam just before she entered, gestured for her to sit in the chair not far from the bed, an antique French bergère cushioned with white silk tweed, piped and braided with emerald green, the room's accent colour.

When she could speak, she asked, "How would you like to spend Christmas cruising in the Caribbean? This" — waving a single sheet of expensive laid paper — "is a letter from Arianna Dracoulis, inviting me to spend Christmas on her father's yacht — and to bring a friend with me."

Katy knew that Arianna, daughter of the Greek shipping magnate, was one of Thalia's best customers and advertisements, and that they were on friendly terms.

"By 'a friend', I expect she means Philip," she suggested.

"Yes, probably, but I'm getting a little bored with Philip, and would rather take you. I may meet someone new," said Thalia. "I know you were used to the high life while your father was alive, Katy, but not on the *grande luxe* scale of Andreas Dracoulis's life-style. It's an experience you shouldn't turn down, even if Robert doesn't approve."

"I should love to go with you," Katy agreed. "But shouldn't I be out of place? Surely everyone else will be members of the jet set, or film stars, or famous, as you are."

"A beautiful girl is never out of place anywhere, and you are a beauty, Katy, although you take your looks lightly. I shall never know why you chose cookery when you could have been a model or an actress."

The answer to that was that Katy had taken her cookery course because, when their marriage was breaking up, Charles had said to her, "I wouldn't have believed any girl of reasonable intelligence could be so useless in the galley. You can't even fry an egg properly."

"I never expected to have to," had been her angry retort. For, at the time, she had resented having to wait on the passengers who had chartered the sloop for a holiday.

Later, when she had grown up and become a sensible adult instead of a spoilt little girl, she had been ashamed of her incompetence, and determined that if ever she and Charles should meet again, she would be as capable of producing an appetising meal as he had been.

He was in her mind most of the day, as he had not been for a long time. At first, she remembered, they had been very happy together, until shortage of money had made it necessary to turn to chartering for a living, and then their troubles had begun. If the charterers had always been nice, well-mannered, considerate people, perhaps she might have adapted to spending at least half the day in the rôle of waitress-cum-chambermaid. One party of charterers were nice; a London doctor and his wife, and their two teenage children. They had made up their bunks every morning, and left the washroom in order, and behaved in a civilised manner which had made it a pleasure to have them aboard. But others had shared her own father's cavalier attitude to employees and, much as Katy disliked it when her father treated people rudely, she disliked it a great deal more when she was being given orders without a please or a thank-you, or when she found the handbasin full of hairs, or the heads in a repugnant condition.

If Charles had sympathised with her, she could have borne it more equably. But he had taken the attitude that a great many people bore worse burdens than hers, and she ought to be counting her blessings, not moaning about trivial pinpricks.

He had assumed, incorrectly, that she had learned to cook at her finishing school. Had she done so, instead of taking an alternative course, their marriage might have survived, as he would then have done the cleaning and she the catering. But he had not the time to be helmsman, and cook, and cabin steward, and her attempts to provide meals, if not completely uneatable, were far below the standard their passengers could be expected to accept. So Charles had taken over the cooking and marketing, in addition to his other responsibilities, and she had been left with the menial jobs which, in her youthful self-centredness, she had felt unfair and beneath her, never stopping to think that there were many girls in the world who, for nights of love in the arms of a man like her husband, would have thought her duties a sinecure.

The final straw had been when one of the charterers, a middle-aged man with yellow teeth and grubby nails, had started slyly to fondle her. She had not dared to tell Charles as, although she had never seen his temper, she felt sure he had one, and might, if he lost it, endanger his livelihood.

What agency would take bookings for a boat whose skipper had been sued for assault? So she had endured having her bottom pinched, and the two or three furtive embraces which her tormentor had forced on her. And at the end of that charter she had gone back to the villa for a few days' break, and had lingered there for a fortnight until Charles had come to fetch her.

She had felt sure that he would come, if she stayed away from him long enough; and that, in the light of the difficulties of their first charter season, he would accept the job which her father was prepared to offer him. By now Howard White had accepted their marriage as a fait accompli, and was only concerned to increase her comfort.

But on that score she had been proved wrong. She had found that Charles would not admit that the season had been the disaster it had seemed to her. He said they had earned enough money to keep them through the winter, if they lived frugally, and he told her he had no intention of becoming her father's hireling — ever. When she had jibbed at going back with him to the port where the sloop was berthed, she had half hoped, deep down, he would make her.

But he had only shrugged, and said mockingly, "Stay here then, if you want to. But you'll come back sooner or later . . . when you're tired of sleeping alone . . . when you're hungry for this."

He had put his arms round her and kissed her, and she had melted against him, quivering with longing to feel those skilful caresses which excited her beyond bearing. But he had not stayed to make love to her, but had left her frustrated and angry because she knew he had done it deliberately, confident that she could not resist his power over her. So, like a fool, she had resisted; fighting her longing for his arms, determined to make him surrender to his need for her.

Which he had. Six weeks later, in the middle of the night, he had come through her bedroom window and woken her out of what she had thought was a dream into the panting reality of the most passionate fusion they had ever experienced.

But it had been an empty victory. In the morning, she found he had gone, leaving a note to her scrawled on the pad on her writing table. He would come to her sometimes, when it suited him. But if she wanted to live with him, it had to be his way, not hers. He would never work for her father. She could share his life only on his terms.

When Robert fetched Katy that evening, she had already cooked their supper which, in foil-covered dishes, needed only to be re-heated in the oven at his flat.

She had meant to restrain her curiosity until they arrived there, but found she could not wait to hear what, if anything, he had found out; not about the divorce regulations, but about her estranged husband.

"Any news, Robert?" she asked.

"Not much, I'm afraid. My solicitor is away from the office at present, and rather than consult anyone else I'll let it hang fire for a week until he comes back."

"And your other enquiry?" she prompted, when he did not immediately refer to it.

"I didn't get far with that either. Ormond's boat changed hands two years ago. She belongs to someone in the Pacific now.

I've cabled the present owner to find out if he knows where we might contact Ormond, but it isn't likely that he will."

"So Charles went back to the Pacific," she said, speaking half to herself. "He said he would, when he could afford it. He told me one could spend a lifetime exploring those islands."

"It's a great place for beachcombing, I believe," he remarked, in a rather scathing tone.

"Charles wasn't a shiftless sort of person," she found herself saying defensively.

"He wasn't particularly responsible if he gave up a career in the Navy to sail round the world, which even women can do now."

The hint of patronage in the phrase 'even women' made her hackles rise slightly.

They stopped at traffic lights, and Robert turned his head to look at her. "You don't still care for him, surely?"

Katy sighed, and averted her face. "I don't know, Robert. I suppose, if one has been married to someone, one can never entirely forget them. But I was so young when I knew him, and he was the kind of man who throws women off their balance. Perhaps what I felt wasn't love. Perhaps it was only attraction . . . physical attraction."

But even as she said it, she remembered the other things she and Charles had had in common. Music. Swimming. Certain kinds of jokes.

To change the subject, she said, "Thalia has been invited to spend Christmas on Andreas Dracoulis's yacht in the Caribbean. She wants me to go with her."

"Must you?"

"I don't *have* to if I don't want to, but I do want. Robert, who wouldn't?"

"I can't say that I should care for it. I always spend Christmas at home with the rest of the family." He had a brother and two sisters, and several nephews and nieces.

"That must be very enjoyable . . . a family Christmas in the house where you grew up. But as I haven't a family, I shall enjoy being with Thalia, and sampling the ultimate flesh-pots."

"If it hadn't been for all these unforeseen complications, I had hoped you would share our Christmas," he said, sounding rather aggrieved.

40

His mood improved during dinner. "You really are a wonderful cook," he said, as they washed up the dishes.

Later on, had she been willing, she was fairly certain that, in spite of his scruples the night before, he would have made love to her. But whereas yesterday she had been willing, tonight she was not, and before his kisses became too heated, she gently extricated herself and asked him to take her home.

"I wish you hadn't accepted this invitation from Dracoulis," Robert said in the car.

"It wasn't from Mr Dracoulis, but from his daughter Arianna. She's been buying Thalia's clothes since her seventeenth birthday, three years ago."

"I don't like the idea of your being involved with those kind of people."

"What do you mean — 'those kind of people'?"

"They're not normal, very rich people. They change their wives more often than ordinary people change the wallpaper. Their values are different," he answered.

"My father's values were different. I don't think I'm likely to be corrupted by Mr Dracoulis or his daughter."

41

"Corrupted, no. But you might find their milieu distasteful."

"I should think I would find it intensely interesting. Andreas Dracoulis would fascinate anyone, surely? Wouldn't you like to meet him?"

"Yes, I suppose I should," he admitted. "But I'm not a woman. He has a bad record with women."

"But he's had, and still has, the pick of all the most stunning beauties. I think it's very unlikely he'll take much notice of me."

The next night Thalia gave a party for thirty, and the night after that a small dinner party. It was three days before Katy saw Robert again. In the meantime she had thought carefully about his proposal, and realised Thalia was right. She did not want to be his wife. There were various differences of outlook which did not matter in a love affair, but which could undermine a marriage.

To let him down lightly, the next time they met she suggested they should not see each other again until after Christmas; separation being the best test of their feelings for each other. With reluctance Robert accepted this. He had already received a reply to his cable to the Pacific. The present owner of the sloop had no knowledge of Charles Ormond's whereabouts. Although Robert had not yet been able to consult his solicitor, he seemed to feel that arranging to divorce a man who might be anywhere in the world was likely to be a long and complex operation.

Five days before Christmas, Thalia and Katy flew from London to Barbados, and then to Tobago where they were met by a hired car in which they were driven across the island to the bay where the Dracoulis yacht was lying at anchor in deep water. A tender was moored to a jetty, waiting to take them and their luggage alongside the gleaming white vessel, and Arianna Dracoulis, a slender, dark-haired girl in white shorts and a turquoise halter, was waiting to greet them at the head of the gangway.

She was said to be the image of her mother, the Greek millionaire's first wife, whom he had married when he was only eighteen and to whom, according to legend, he would be married still, had she not been killed in an air crash. Since then he had had two more marriages of only a few years' duration, and his name had been linked with half a dozen other beautiful women.

"Thalia! How nice to see you. Did you have a smooth flight?" asked the Greek girl, taking her guest by both hands and leaning forward to kiss her, first on one cheek and then the other. "And this is your friend Miss Brown. How do you do? Welcome aboard" — this greeting accompanied by a more restrained handshake but a very warm smile which made Katy feel truly welcome.

"I'm sure the first thing you'd like is a long cold drink and a shower. Come, let me show you your cabins. We shall be a party of twelve, but as yet only three of our other guests have arrived. You can meet them later, when you have rested and changed. Papa is busy, as always. He will join us for drinks before dinner."

So it was that within fifteen minutes of setting foot on the deck of *Artemis* — named after Arianna's mother — Katy found herself lying in a warm bath, sipping a drink called a Perroquet which Arianna had made for her from one part Pernod to five parts of iced soda water, with a dash of crême de menthe to give it a pale emerald tinge. The makings of this had come from a well-stocked drinks cupboard and a refrigerator concealed in the wood-panelled walls of Katy's cabin where, while she relaxed in the bath, a stewardess was unpacking her suitcases.

The cases were good ones, from Hermès, two relics of her moneyed past, as were some of the things they contained — a pair of white silk pyjamas her father had bought her from Fortnum & Mason, a dark red leather belt from the Yves Saint Laurent boutique, and other undating accessories which gave a touch of luxury to her otherwise tight-budget wardrobe.

At one time she would have minded that the stewardess might think it strange for any guest on *Artemis* to have so many cheap clothes. Now Katy knew that expensive clothes were the least important weapons in a woman's armoury because, although other women might notice them, few men would recognise the difference between *haute couture* and C & A; and if the women she was going to meet on this cruise thought any the less of her, she was long past being crushed or upset by such shallow attitudes.

Presently, wrapped in the white towelling robe and matching mules put out for her use, she went through to the cabin to find the stewardess stowing the emptied cases in a compartment at the top of the built-in cupboards which had doors faced with mirror-glass to make the cabin seem more spacious, although by comparison with Charles's sloop, her quarters here seemed palatial.

"What will you wear for dinner tonight, Miss Brown?" the stewardess enquired.

"What sort of thing would you suggest? Will it be formal?"

"No, quite informal, I should think, miss. Later on, when the other ladies and gentlemen have arrived, I expect the ladies will dress up more, but something such as your lime green trousers and the blouse with a stripe of the same colour would do for this evening."

"Right: I'll wear those," Katy agreed.

"I'll lay them out for you later, miss.

They might need just a little pressing; although, if you don't mind my saying so, if you do your own packing, as many young ladies do now, you do it much better than most."

"Thank you. Yes, I do my own packing, and as I'm sure you're the most expert of packers, I take that as a great compliment," Katy replied, with a smile. "Have you been on *Artemis* long?"

"Oh, yes, ever since her maiden voyage as a yacht, miss. She was a frigate originally. Mr Dracoulis had her completely refitted for the first Mrs Dracoulis. Such a lovely lady, she was. It was a terrible tragedy when she was killed so soon afterwards. There's never been another to touch her. Well, if you've everything you need for the moment, I'll leave you, but if you want me for anything, just press that bell by the bed."

"Thank you." Katy had the impression the stewardess regretted her last remark concerning the owner's first wife. She was probably a natural chatterbox who had to restrain a tendency to gossip.

A few moments after her departure Thalia appeared, wearing a sleek black swimsuit under a black and white wrap. She had taken, and insisted on Katy taking it with her, a course of solarium treatments, so that both of them had a light tan.

"Otherwise we shall look unappetizingly pallid among all the others who will doubtlessly be the types to have an all-the-year-round tan," she had said, before their first dose of artificial sunlight.

Now she said, "Shall we go to the pool, and see who else is here?"

"Yes, as soon as I can find my bikinis," said Katy, searching the drawers and eventually finding her four newly-bought bathing suits.

Her holidays since leaving Spain after the final break with Charles had been spent in the English countryside, and it was four years since she had done any swimming. The many bikinis and one-piece *maillots* which she had owned before then had been left behind at the villa, and thrown out when it was sold and the proceeds used to pay the heavy fines her father had incurred as a result of his currency fiddles.

From the four new bikinis she chose one of sky-blue cotton patterned with sprawling white flowers. Watching her as she put it on, Thalia said, "I wish I had your curves. It's fine being thin when one's dressed, but not so good when one's not."

They found their way to the pool deck where, as they walked along the edge of the glinting rectangle of water to the group reclining on loungers at the far end, Katy recognised the famous features of Carly Martin, the actress, who had shed the top of her bikini and from the hips up was covered only by a film of sun-oil.

"I'm not baring *my* bosom, what little there is of it," murmured Thalia, in an undertone, before they came within earshot.

The other early arrivals were a husband and wife, he an American architect and she the head of her own public relations firm in New York. She and Thalia seemed to feel an instant rapport, but as soon as she could Katy excused herself from a conversation with the others and went to dive into the pool.

She swam up and down several times, then turned on her back and floated with arms outflung and the sunlight warm on her face. This was not like the heavily chlorinated pools in which she had never liked swimming. This was salt water, pumped out of the sea, and as invigorating as the sea. She began to swim back and forth again, feeling her whole body stretched and revitalised by the exercise she liked better than any other, and which she had missed more than she knew.

At length, feeling it might be impolite to stay in too long by herself, she swung herself out by the steps at the end furthest from the others. On the non-slip surround, she paused to rake back her long streaming hair and to wipe the water out of her eyes.

She gave a deep sigh of pleasure. "Mm . . . lovely," she murmured aloud.

"I agree," said a voice from behind her.

Turning, she found herself looking into the smiling dark eyes of a man who, even if she had never seen a picture of him, she would have known could only be Andreas Dracoulis.

He was the same height as she was; small for a man, but thickset, with powerful shoulders and hair the colour of steel wool, although thick and smooth in texture.

50

He was twenty years older than she, but he emanated the vitality of a much younger man.

"Lovely indeed, Miss Katy Brown," he said, as he looked her over in a frank appraisal of her figure which somehow was not offensive, as it might have been from someone else.

"How do you do, Mr Dracoulis." She held out her hand, and he took it in a strong clasp. "How did you know my name?"

"I know the names of all my guests, and my daughter's guests. You are not Miss Harcourt, of whom I have seen a photograph, so you must be Miss Brown, although I shall call you Katy, if you permit it." His dark brown eyes twinkled at her, and she felt the force of his charm.

He was not quite but almost old enough to be her father, and yet in spite of the age gap, and his short stature, she found him extremely attractive. Only one other man had had the same instant appeal for her, and that had been Charles.

She found it slightly unnerving to be taken by the elbow and steered to the other end of the pool and there, while she towelled her wet hair and blotted her skin, to have him concentrate on her, apparently oblivious to the beautiful golden breasts of the film actress, and the lively, witty conversation of the two successful career-women.

"You seem to have made a hit with our host," said Thalia, later, when they were returning to their cabins to change for dinner.

It crossed Katy's mind that although her friend's tone was light, inwardly she might not be pleased.

"I think he was just being kind to the least distinguished of his guests. He probably realised that I might be conscious of my ordinariness in such scintillating company," said Katy.

"As I've told you before, you underrate yourself, sweetie. Carly Martin has nothing that you haven't got, except that she flaunts hers more freely. If you can nobble Andreas, you go right ahead. He's a remarkable man. Six months with him would be as interesting and memorable as six years with most men," said Thalia.

"Aren't you interested in Mr Dracoulis?" asked Katy.

"No, I don't know why, but he doesn't

switch me on particularly. But there are five more guests arriving tomorrow, and one of them may be my type."

The five guests already on board had been asked to assemble for drinks in the main saloon about eight and, as Katy's stewardess had forecast, no one was formally dressed. Andreas Dracoulis wore a cotton shirt, batik-patterned in brown, black and fudge, over a pair of white trousers, and Arianna appeared in cyclamen pants and a shirt of pale Indian silk.

At first the women outnumbered the men by five to two, but Katy heard their host telling the American women that they would be joined shortly by his captain and the first officer.

Katy and Thalia were strolling about, studying the magnificent paintings which adorned the wood-panelled bulkheads, when the two ship's officers arrived to better the balance of the sexes.

The first to enter was the captain, a grey-bearded man in his fifties, wearing a naval-style uniform of crisply-laundered white drill with dark blue tabs on his shoulders, white shorts, and white stockings and shoes.

He was followed by his second in command, a much taller and younger man in a similar uniform but without the two rows of medal ribbons which were pinned to the captain's burly chest.

"Now that's for me . . . oh, yes, definitely," Thalia murmured in Katy's ear, as the taller man entered, a few steps behind his superior.

Katy drew in a sharp, startled breath, and the room seemed to spin for a moment as she stared with disbelieving eyes at the bronzed, rawboned, arrogant face of the man to whom she was still, officially, married.

2

ANDREAS went round the room, introducing the two officers to his guests. Thalia and Katy were the last to meet them.

"Miss Harcourt, may I present the Master of my yacht, Commander John Longhurst, formerly of the Royal Navy, and also our First Officer, Mr Charles Ormond. Miss Harcourt is one of London's leading dress designers, and this is her friend, Miss Katy Brown," he told the two men.

Katy watched them shake hands with Thalia. She knew Charles had already caught sight of her, but he had not betrayed his shock as much as she feared she had done. Only the raising of one dark eyebrow might have suggested to a close observer that the sight of her had come as a slight surprise to him.

The Commander took her hand in his. "Good evening, Miss Brown. Have you been to this part of the world before?"

"No, never."

Her throat contracted, her mouth became suddenly dry as the moment came for Charles to shake hands with her.

"Miss . . . Brown?" he said interrogatively, as if he were not quite sure he had her name correctly.

"Yes . . . without an e. How do you do, Mr Ormond." It amazed her that she could speak calmly when her heart was pounding so violently.

Four years had changed him, she saw. His grey eyes were harder, his mouth had a cynical tilt. He was more attractive than ever. She could see why Thalia was smitten.

He turned back to chat to the designer, and Katy said to Commander Longhurst, "You know these islands well, I expect?"

"Yes, this is not our first cruise in the Caribbean. When all the guests have arrived, we're going further north, to the Granadines."

"That's where Princess Margaret has a holiday home, isn't it?"

"I believe it is."

They went on making polite small-talk, with Katy trying not to listen to the conversation of the other two. The party was not yet complete. Shortly before they had dinner, a guest from the island came on board, an internationally-known artist who had come to live in Tobago to combat chronic bronchitis.

At dinner Andreas Dracoulis sat at the head of the table with his daughter at the foot, and the American woman and Carly Martin on his right and left. Next to Carly was seated the artist, with Katy between him and the Master. Thalia was opposite her, between Charles and the architect.

This arrangement gave Katy an excellent view of her husband whose glance rested briefly upon her as he held Thalia's chair for her, and the artist attended to Katy.

What was he thinking? she wondered. Was anything left of his love for her? Or had she completely killed it by her immaturity and obstinacy? Surely, if he had had any vestige of feeling left for her after their separation, he would have come to her aid when her father was taken into custody, and her world had collapsed overnight as if in an earthquake?

She had never seen Thalia more sparkling. Clearly, she would have monopolised

Charles throughout the meal, ignoring the architect, which would not have mattered greatly as he had Arianna to talk to and also, the table being a large oval, Commander Longhurst. But it would have been a breach of good manners and, although it might be that Charles also would have preferred to concentrate his attention on Thalia, he was more punctilious than she. After a time he turned to make conversation to the woman on the other side of him.

For her part, Katy was careful not to glance at him too often, in which she was helped by the artist, who was an animated man with a fund of amusing stories. She had been listening to one of these and, at the end of it, had broken into soft laughter, when she turned her head and found Charles's gaze fixed on her face. There was a strange look in his eyes which she could not interpret. The smile left her lips. She felt herself starting to flush, and quickly looked down at the crab-back which had just been served to her.

Did he hate her now? Was that the emotion behind that enigmatic look?

Coffee was taken on deck, under a sky blazing with stars. Having drunk his coffee while in conversation with Carly Martin, who tonight was in a black shirt and tight white silk pants, the First Officer disappeared, presumably to attend to some matter of ship's routine.

Katy would have liked to go to her cabin and be alone, but she felt it might seem ungracious to excuse herself too early. Fortunately it was not long before Arianna suggested that, having had a long day, she and Thalia might like an early night.

"We shall be at anchor most of tomorrow, waiting for the others to fly in, so if you feel like staying in bed until lunch-time, please do," she told them. "We like everyone to relax in their own way, which for some people means getting up early and spending the morning water-skiing, and for others is lazing all day and coming to life in the evening. If you want breakfast at six a.m. there will be someone on duty to bring it to you. Do just as you like."

"I certainly shan't be ringing for breakfast at six a.m.," said Thalia, yawning, after they had said goodnight and were going below. "Flying always knocks the stuffing out of me, and the chief attraction having gone on watch, or whatever, I may as well fall into bed. Rather a dish, the First Officer, don't you think? Well, actually I hope you don't. It wouldn't do for us both to fancy him."

"Is it 'done' to flirt with the crew?" Katy asked lightly.

Thalia laughed. "My dear, when did I ever care what was 'done' or not? If Dracoulis doesn't want his crew flirted with, as you so delicately phrase it, he shouldn't employ such tempting hunks of masculinity."

"Mr Ormond may be a married man."

"Yes, he is — I asked him that. Never let it be said that I filch other women's husbands."

"But you're going to filch this one, I gather."

"His wife doesn't want him, or he doesn't want her. He didn't go into details, thank goodness; there's really nothing more boring than the history of someone's broken marriage. Charles just said that he was married but separated.

What a fool of a girl to let go of someone like him!"

Katy wondered what Thalia would say if she answered, "Yes, wasn't I?" Ought she to tell her that she was the girl in the case?

She hesitated, decided she needed to sleep on it, and said, "It must be a difficult life, being married to a man whose job takes him away for long periods."

"Yes, it must, but in this case I should think he could have had her on board with him. I know that on some of those vast oil tankers they build now, there's accommodation for wives."

"Is there?" Katy said vaguely. They had reached the door of her cabin, and she was on the point of saying goodnight, when Thalia said, "Shall I come in for a nightcap?" to which the only possible reply seemed to be, "Yes, do."

"My goodness, the paintings on this yacht must be worth a million!" exclaimed the designer, beginning to look at the various pictures in Katy's quarters. "I've got a Cézanne in my cabin, would you believe? And this one looks like a Zoffany.

Yes, it is" — this last remark as the engraving on a discreet strip of gilt-metal attached to the bottom of the frame confirmed her judgment.

"I like those watercolours best," said Katy, relieved that Thalia's thoughts had taken another direction, and hoping her friend would not mention Charles again.

Thalia studied the two Turner sketches which hung near the bed, then sat down in a comfortable chair and agreed with Katy's suggestion that a little white rum would be an appropriate nightcap.

"Oh, no — I didn't mean neat, sweetie," she said, when Katy handed her a small measure. "Some tonic and ice with mine, please."

Foreseeing that, in spite of her claim to be tired, Thalia intended to stay for at least half an hour of chatter, Katy dropped some ice into tall glasses and re-poured the rum from the small glasses she had selected before.

"When I first saw her by the pool this afternoon, I thought Carly Martin must be Dracoulis's latest girlfriend. But although she sat next to him at dinner, I'm not sure now that she is. His manner towards her was pleasant, but not at all amorous," said Thalia, lighting a cigarette.

Katy, a non-smoker, felt a flicker of vexation at having her sleeping quarters filled with smoke at bedtime.

Aloud, she said, "Perhaps he prefers to be amorous in private."

Thalia gave her a sharp glance. "Is that an oblique dig at me for letting my yen for Charles show?"

"No, it wasn't," Katy said truthfully. It must have been her annoyance about the cigarette smoke which made her remark sound barbed.

"There are two schools of thought on the subject," said Thalia. "You, I know, belong to the one which thinks men should do all the running, and women should only reveal their earthy side after accepting the proposal — or the proposition, as the case may be. I don't see it that way. If I fancy a man, I let him know it, as they do with us. Charles isn't the type to be scared off by a woman looking hungrily at him. Very few men are, in my experience. They're as flattered by it as we are when they look lustfully at us."

"It can be anything but flattering," said Katy, remembering the charter passenger who had, in a way, contributed to the split with Charles, and one or two other men whose advances she had found far from complimentary.

"I may not have a bust like Carly's, but I know I've got something which appeals to the male sex. I don't think Charles is going to sidle away when he sees me coming."

"No, I'm sure he won't," Katy agreed. "But perhaps, among the people who are arriving tomorrow, there may be someone even dishier."

Thalia nodded. "There may be. I meant to ask Arianna who else was coming, but I forgot." She swirled her drink, making the ice cubes clink against the glass. "But Charles suits my mood at the moment. Philip was too super-smooth." Her vivid blue cat's eyes gleamed as she smiled to herself. "I suspect the First Officer of having a primitive streak beneath that suave social manner. What do you think?"

"I think a ten-day cruise is rather a short time to get involved with someone whose life-style doesn't fit in with yours," Katy responded. "Won't it interfere with your work if he gets under your skin, and you have to go back to London and not see him any more?"

"Maybe I'll get under *his* skin, and he'll change his life-style," was the designer's careless reply.

"Oh, Thalia, that would be cruel — to make him give up what must be an excellent post of the kind he might not get again. Anyway, I'm sure he wouldn't. Commander Longhurst probably retires at sixty, and Mr Ormond must be in line for his job. He doesn't look the kind of man who would sacrifice that prospect for any woman, however attractive."

"No, I think you're right there," Thalia conceded. "He doesn't, does he? In fact he looks to me like a thoroughly reactionary dominant male who, if he was serious about anyone, would expect her to drop everything — her career, her friends, all her interests — and re-shape her life to suit him. Maybe that's why his marriage broke up. Maybe the ex-wife liked being dominated in bed, but she wasn't too keen on the role of little woman out of bed."

"Perhaps. Who can say?" answered Katy. "Thalia, I'm drooping with tiredness. Would you mind if I turned you out now? I really can hardly keep my eyes open."

"You do look rather bushed." Thalia crushed out her cigarette. "See you some time tomorrow. What time I'll get up, I don't know. Let's take Arianna's advice and each do our own thing, shall we? 'Night-night."

"Goodnight."

When she was alone, Katy tipped the cigarette ash into the lavatory and washed the hand-painted Limoges porcelain ash tray so as not to wake up to the unpleasant smell of stale tobacco. By the time she had taken off her make-up and brushed her teeth, most of the smoke had wafted out of the wide-open ports.

The bed had been turned down while she was out of the cabin. The sheets and pillow-cases were pale green, and there was a light blanket of the same delicate shade folded at the foot of the bed. Katy slid under the top sheet. In a recessed shelf behind the night table was a selection of new books which, in other circumstances would have kept her lamp alight until the small hours. Tonight, although not really sleepy as she had professed, she was not in the mood to read. She wanted to lie in the dark and recover from the shock of meeting Charles.

In fact when she switched off the light, the cabin was not left in darkness but in moonglow. She lay with her eyes wide open, and her arms upflung on the pillow, and wondered if Charles had disappeared, not because he had duties to attend to, but because he, too, was knocked sideways by this unexpected encounter.

Not that he had appeared to be knocked sideways, but then neither had she, after the first few seconds of stunned stupefaction when he had walked into the saloon behind Commander Longhurst.

"You don't still care for him, surely?" Robert Otterway had asked her.

At the time she hadn't been sure. Now she was. From the instant she had set eyes on Charles, she had known that he had been and was still the only man in the world for her.

Dear God! What a situation, she thought, with a lump in her throat. Me loving Charles. Him, perhaps, loathing me. And the woman I work for — my friend — wanting to jump into bed with him. Not an ideal set-up for a pleasure cruise, or a merry Christmas!

When she opened her eyes the next morning, the cabin was full of dancing sea-lights. The flat calm of the night before had given place to a slightly breeze-ruffled surface which caused the shimmering reflections which she had not seen since the last time she had awoken aboard Charles's sloop.

Charles! The thought of him made her heart lurch as she remembered that he was no longer part of her past but, if only for the next ten days, part of her present. Could she, in that short time, reanimate the love he had felt for her once? Had they a future together? It didn't seem likely, but she had to try. She must try.

Within ten minutes of waking she was on deck, by the pool. It was not yet seven o'clock and no one else was about. Dropping the towelling robe she had brought from her bathroom on the end of a lounger, she dived in and swam back and forth, counting the lengths until she reached thirty. She was treading water for a few minutes, debating whether to push her target up to fifty, when a voice said, "Good morning . . . Miss Brown."

Turning her head, she saw Charles standing at the pool's edge, his arms folded across his chest. He was in uniform, with the addition of a peaked hat.

"Good morning." She swam to the steps and climbed out.

As she walked towards him he saluted, a formal gesture at variance with his expression. Slowly his grey gaze travelled over her figure in a leisurely and intimate inspection of the body which once had been his to touch and caress.

He was standing close to the lounger where she had left the robe and, as she reached for it, he forestalled her.

"Allow me . . . Miss Brown." He held it for her to slip her arms into the sleeves, his expression mocking, as if he knew that her self-possession was as fragile as spun sugar.

"You appear to be a keen swimmer

. . . Miss Brown."

"Don't taunt me, Charles," she said, in a low, pleading voice. "I had to adopt the name Brown after my father was sent to prison. You don't know how the press can hound one. Perhaps you don't even know that he was imprisoned?"

"I didn't know at the time. I heard about it later. But your name wasn't White, so why should anyone have associated you with him?" he asked sardonically.

Katy knotted the sash of the robe and thrust her hands into the pockets. "I — I reverted to White after we separated. Anyway, I shouldn't have thought you would have been pleased to have your name dragged through all that mud, as it would have been had I still been known as Mrs Ormond. Fortunately nobody knew of your connection with us."

He seemed about to reply, then changed his mind and said, as if they were strangers, "You'll have to excuse me . . . Miss Brown. I have things which demand my attention."

He turned on his heel and strode away, his long legs as brown as an islander's between his white shorts and the tops of the white cotton sockings which set off his muscular calves and lean, shapely ankles.

Katy sat down on the lounger, closing her eyes against the rush of hot tears which had glazed her vision as she watched him depart.

After a minute or two she pulled herself together and went to lean on the rail, gazing at the steep wooded heights of the island half a mile inshore.

She was still there, musing, when Andreas Dracoulis came to her side.

"Are you always an early riser, Katy?"

"Usually. Are you?"

He nodded. "But I need only four hours' sleep, so I burn my candle at both ends. Would you care to have breakfast with me?"

"With pleasure, Mr Dracoulis."

"Andreas."

"Andreas," she repeated. She found it hard to believe that she was here, on this huge sixteen-hundred-ton yacht, calling this extraordinary man — who mixed with royalty and presidents — by his first name.

He took her, by a staircase walled with illuminated showcases containing all kinds of beautiful objects which had caught his fancy, to his private quarters on the bridge deck. Outside the sliding glass doors of his study was a deck like a balcony, overlooking the whole after part of the vessel, including the pool. A breakfast table, laid for two, awaited them.

"I am having devilled kidneys this morning. Do you like them, or would you prefer something else?" he asked, having drawn out a chair for her.

"I like them very much."

"And orange juice first?"

"Yes, please."

He pressed a bell and, when a steward appeared, told the man that Miss Brown would have the same breakfast as himself.

"I've only just realised — you've got an aeroplane on board!" Katy exclaimed, looking at the small scarlet aircraft which could only be seen from this vantage point. "But how does it take off and land?"

"She's an amphibian. When she lands

at sea, our crane raises her to deck-level. We also have a car on board. *Artemis* is fully equipped for all contingencies. If you should be taken ill — most unlikely, you look a very healthy young woman — we have our own ship's hospital with X-ray and surgical facilities."

She took her first sip of the orange juice without actually looking at it, her eyes fixed on the face of her host as, with open pride, he listed some of the yacht's other amenities, including a radio office which kept him in touch with all parts of the world by signal and, within a lesser radius, by radio telephone. Then the taste of the juice made her glance at the graceful glass goblet she held in her hand, and she realised that what she was drinking was orange juice and champagne.

She had had something like it before when, at the villa in Spain, her father had added Spanish bubbly to orange juice to make Buck's Fizz as a pre-luncheon drink. But never before had she drunk French champagne before breakfast.

Andreas was not a man obsessed by his own affairs, and his seemingly genuine interest in her was balm after Charles's rebuff. They were at the coffee and croissant stage when it flashed through her mind that, had Charles not existed, she could easily have fallen in love with this small, dynamic Greek genius. Which would have involved her, no doubt, in even more heartache than she had suffered already, she thought wryly.

"So you are an old-fashioned girl who likes to cook and keep house," he said, having learned that her relationship with Thalia was not one of friendship alone. "My wife was the same — my first wife. She would not have cared if I had remained as poor as I was when we married. That isn't to say that she did not enjoy the fruits of my success, but she would have been equally happy had we had to remain in modest circumstances. Arianna is very much like her in looks, but not in character. My daughter has her mother's warm heart, but she is too easily bored. I'm afraid I have spoilt her."

"She doesn't strike me as being spoilt," said Katy. "When I was her age, I was horribly spoilt, but I've grown out of it."

"Ah, but I think life has hurt you. You have known what it is to be unhappy? Am I right?"

"Yes ... for a while," she admitted. "I – I lost my father in particularly painful circumstances, but at least it made me grow up and see life from a more sensible perspective."

She smiled at him, adding, with less than perfect truth, "And I'm certainly not unhappy now. How could I be? – In this beautiful part of the world, after starting the day with a swim and a delicious breakfast with someone I never expected to have the pleasure of meeting."

He returned her smile. "These surroundings may be adjuncts to happiness. They are not its essence."

"What is its essence, do you think?"

"Two things. A satisfying occupation, and a good relationship with one's husband or wife. I should not care to say which I think the more important of the two. Certainly, to live well one must have one or the other. To have both, as I did for a time, is to savour life to the full."

He finished his third cup of coffee and

tossed his napkin on the table. "Would it interest you to visit the bridge?"

"Yes, very much." Would Charles be there? she wondered, with mingled anticipation and apprehension.

But they had the yacht's bridge to themselves. Neither the Captain nor his First Officer were there, and she realised that they would scarcely be likely to spend much time there while the yacht was at anchor.

Andreas knew the function of all the complex pieces of equipment with which the bridge was fitted. Katy listened attentively while he explained them to her.

"You mentioned last night that Commander Longhurst was formerly in the Royal Navy," she remarked presently. "Is Mr Ormond also an ex-Naval officer?"

"Yes, but with only a few years' service, whereas John had half a lifetime of Naval service behind him when I persuaded him to take command of my yacht. Ormond's father was his contemporary, and served with him during the Second World War, only to be killed on land a few years after it.

The boy was brought up by his grandfather, Admiral Ormond. Charles isn't a man who talks about himself, but I gather he didn't really want to go into the Navy and did so to please his grandfather. When the old man died, he left the Service and spent the next year emulating Sir Francis Chichester and all the other single-handed circumnavigators."

"How did he come to be your First Officer?" Katy asked.

She was half afraid that Andreas was so acute that he would detect that her interest in his second in command was not as casual as she wanted it to seem. But at the same time she could not resist her curiosity.

"We were cruising in the Pacific," said her host. "I saw him perform an act of remarkable courage when there was an outbreak of fire on a small yacht berthed near the sloop which he owned at that time. At great risk to himself, he rescued a child trapped on board. They were both burned, although not severely, and we brought them aboard *Artemis* to be treated by my Medical Officer. Naturally the name Ormond alerted John's interest, and he soon found out that this was the son of his friend. As John had retired from the Navy at the same time that Charles had joined it, they had never come across each other. It wasn't long before both John and I had formed the opinion that here was a man of quite exceptional calibre whose abilities were not fully extended. He seemed to have had his fill of exploring the world's oceans, but not to have anything else in mind. I offered him a position on *Artemis* which he accepted. When the previous First Officer left us, Ormond replaced him. He's an excellent officer to whom I would confidently entrust my life, should the situation arise. But I wouldn't vouch for his trustworthiness with your sex. If, as I surmised at dinner last night, your friend Thalia has her eye on him, I think she ought to be warned that he's something of a pirate where women are concerned."

"Mr Ormond told her he was married, but not living with his wife."

"Perhaps his experience of marriage is the cause of his present attitude to women," suggested Andreas. "He amuses himself with them occasionally — and some of my guests are very willing to amuse him," he interpolated dryly, "but I don't think he ever feels the slightest affection for them. However it could be that, in that respect, he and your friend are well matched," he added shrewdly.

"Thalia's greatest interest in life is her work, and it's much more demanding than it might sound," Katy said evasively.

A steward came in with a message on a silver salver.

Andreas said, "Excuse me," and scanned it. "I'm afraid I must leave you for a while."

"May I stay up here for a short time?"

"By all means. We'll meet at lunch." With a smile, he departed to deal with whatever matter of business required his attention.

Left alone on the bridge, Katy thought over what he had told her about Charles. It didn't surprise her that he was the grandson of an Admiral, or that he was capable of bravery. Nor had it come as a surprise to hear that his life since their parting had not been as chaste as hers. Yet it hurt her terribly to think of him making love to other women.

"What are you doing here?"

The familiar voice, not friendly as it had once been, but clipped and hostile, made her jump, startled out of her thoughts of him.

Turning to face Charles, she said, "Mr Dracoulis brought me . . . and then he was called away."

"Now you've seen the bridge; perhaps you'd like me to direct you back to the passengers' part of the ship," he said coldly.

"In a minute. Charles, we must talk."

"Must we? Why?" His eyes were arctic.

"Because . . . oh, Charles, we were married. For a time we were happy together. Is there nothing left now but enmity?"

"Not enmity, merely indifference. Four years is a long time . . . Miss Brown. As they say, time heals all wounds."

"Oh, don't keep calling me Miss Brown in that sarcastic tone," she said distressfully.

"To address you by your correct title would complicate both our lives," he answered.

"Why not call me Katy?"

He shrugged. "If you insist."

Her mouth quivered. "You hate me,

don't you? Well, I deserve it, I know. But I was so — "

Before she could add 'young and foolish', he cut in abruptly, "On the contrary, I'm pleased to find you've fallen on your feet. I thought what happened to your father might have left you in considerable difficulties. But it seems you've survived very well. If you're worried that my presence on board may disrupt your plans, forget it. I shan't interfere. Live and let live is my motto."

"My plans? What plans? I don't understand you," she said.

"Be naïve, if you feel it suits you — but don't think I am," he told her cuttingly. "Like ninety per cent of the females who come aboard *Artemis*, you fancy your chances with Dracoulis. If I were a betting man, I'd put my money on Carly Martin. Maybe I'm wrong. Maybe he'll like that misleadingly innocent air which you've somehow managed to retain. If you beat Miss Martin, good luck to you. Dracoulis's girl-friends seldom last more than three months, and as soon as this cruise is over he'll be living ashore for a while. So it isn't likely that you and I

81

will see much of each other."

She heard him out, her temper beginning to simmer at an allegation which was totally without foundation.

"How dare you!" she flared, when he had finished. "Nothing could be further from my mind. I came on this cruise simply because Arianna invited Thalia to bring a friend with her, and she chose to ask me. I wanted to see the Caribbean, and to get away from the winter weather in England. You have no right to accuse me of having designs on Mr Dracoulis. It's both absurd and insulting!"

A cynical smile tilted the corners of his mouth. "At the risk of enraging you even more, I'd say your friend Thalia is an amoral bitch who will jump into bed with anyone who takes her fancy. If you want to be thought above reproach, you should be more careful of the company you keep. Birds of a feather . . . and so on."

Katy mustered all her self-control to keep her voice low, her delivery calm. "Last night Thalia described you as 'a thoroughly reactionary dominant male'. How right she was! Evidently you haven't realised that the old double standard is finished. You can't any longer condemn women for doing what men have always done — and what I'm quite sure you've done many times in the past four years. Don't tell me that you haven't slept with as many women as would let you?"

His brown face, already hard, seemed to become even harder as the jaw muscles clenched and his level mouth tightened for a moment before he said curtly, "What would you expect? I was never unfaithful to my wife, but when she refused to live with me I saw no reason to live like a monk for the rest of my life."

"Then don't be aspersive about Thalia. It so happens that she has had only one lover in the two years since I met her, and you could be deluding yourself if you fancy your chance of supplanting him."

"She's far too skinny to interest me."

The steward who had brought the message to Andreas reappeared.

"You rang, sir?"

"Yes, Burdon. Would you please show Miss Brown to her quarters. She isn't quite sure of the way."

"Yes, sir."

Without her noticing it, Charles must

have pressed a button to summon the man, and put an end to their tête-à-tête in a way she had no choice but to accept. She moved past him, saying with icy civility, "Thank you, Mr Ormond."

"Not at all."

"Actually I think I'll have another swim before going to my cabin, and I know the way to the pool from here, thank you," she said to the steward, when they had descended two decks.

"Very good, miss."

He had the manner of an English butler, but several of the stewards were Greeks, others French, and some of the seamen she had seen could only be Nordic.

She found the pool still deserted and plunged in to work off her anger with another twenty or thirty lengths. Usually her crawl was leisurely. Now she swam flat out, as if racing. When she finished she was breathless and panting. It was a long time since her days had been spent in and out of the water and, over a short distance only, she could match Charles's powerful strokes.

She no longer had the pool to herself. Carly Martin and Arianna were stretched on loungers, the Greek girl in a minimal saffron bikini and Carly in only a tiny black silk *cache-sexe.* "Are you always so athletic?" she asked, making Katy feel, for a moment, like an over-muscular sports mistress.

"Not always."

Normally Katy would have let the little deliberate pinprick pass. She had no taste for the catty cut-and-thrust which some women seemed to enjoy. But this morning, her usually even temper ruffled by Charles's implication that she had become as amoral as he judged Thalia to be, she felt moved to let Carly know she could, if provoked, thrust and parry.

Smiling at Arianna, she said, "Good morning. Your father has been showing me the bridge, and explaining all the advanced equipment up there. You've seen it too, I expect, Miss Martin? Fascinating, isn't it?"

Carly was oiling her body with sensuous movements of her hands which would have been fascinating to men, but seemed rather wasted on her present companions.

She said, "I'm not much interested in machinery. I was fascinated by the collection of *objets* by Fabergé which Andreas has in his study in his private quarters."

"Yes, I did notice them as we were going on to the balcony for breakfast," Katy riposted casually.

She saw that she had succeeded in annoying Carly, and immediately regretted engaging with her. But for Charles she would not have done; and now here she was behaving as if she *were* in competition with Carly for their host's attention.

In an effort to placate the actress, and make it clear this was not so, she said to Arianna, "It was very kind of your father to invite me to breakfast with him. I'm all too aware that I have very little to contribute to a gathering of brilliant and glamorous people. I'm afraid he must have found my conversation most unscintillating. But it will be something to boast about to my grandchildren, that I once had breakfast with Andreas Dracoulis."

Whether this *amende honorable* succeeded in convincing the actress that Katy was not so vain as to think she could vie with her it was impossible to tell.

Presently Thalia joined them, and asked

Arianna who was arriving that day.

"My uncle Spyros and his wife Marietta; Janus Cator, the film director, and his wife, and a Frenchman, Alain de Noailles," the Greek girl informed her.

Including the two Americans, Taylor and Paulette Stevenson, that made a party of seven women and five men, Katy thought. She guessed the unevenness was caused by Thalia not bringing a man with her. But it could be corrected, as it had the night before, by the inclusion of the two ship's officers in the party.

The first to arrive was the Frenchman who was brought aboard at mid-morning, having come from nearby Trinidad where he had been staying on business. Arianna had said he was a banker, and Katy had hoped he would take Thalia's mind off Charles. But from the moment Arianna introduced him to the group round the pool, it was clear that he had no eyes for any woman but her, and had been invited as her partner. All the other male guests being married — except for their host in whom she seemed uninterested sexually — that left Thalia with no one but Charles to dally with.

The next-comers, just in time for lunch, were Janus Cator and his wife, Valentina, formerly an actress but now in retirement and, at present, seven months pregnant.

When, while they were chatting after lunch, Katy asked if she meant to resume her screen career after the baby was born, Valentina shook her head and gave a very firm negative.

"I'm not Janny's first wife, but I'm determined to be his last one. I love that man," she said, looking tenderly at him as he sat on the edge of the pool, talking to Andreas. "Very few marriages can survive the long separations which occur when people are on different locations, and a man like Janny is constantly beset by lovelies wanting to further their careers."

Her glance rested somewhat speculatively on Carly who, since lunch, had been wearing a vivid cyclamen caftan which, having most of its buttons and loops undone, only half-hid the famous bosom.

However, in spite of the bulge under the emerald cotton skirt of her Empire style maternity swimsuit, Katy thought Valentina had little to fear from a siren like Carly.

Carly belonged to the hardbitten career woman school of stars, but Valentina had been a successor to actresses such as Grace Kelly and Deborah Kerr. Hers was a well-bred beauty, with the added attractions of intelligence and kindness. Carly seemed reasonably intelligent, but Katy had the impression there was very little kindness in her make-up. Ambition was probably the major component in her nature.

"Are you in the theatre in England, Katy?" the film producer asked her, later.

She shook her head.

"You're a model?"

"No, I'm a cook by profession. At present I'm Thalia's housekeeper."

"That seems a waste of a very pretty face and figure."

"Thank you, but you don't count your wife's retirement as a waste, do you? And I'm plain compared with her."

"No, you're right, I don't count it a waste. To tell you the truth, I still can't believe my luck that someone as lovely and talented as Valentina is prepared to give up her career to look after me and my children. But her kind and your kind of women seems to be in danger of extinction.

And you're not a plain girl compared with anyone," he added, with a smile which she recognised as one of detached admiration with no sexual element in it.

She had always enjoyed his films. She began to like Janus more than she would have anticipated liking anyone from the film world. Not that she would have expected Andreas to include anyone too brash in his Christmas cruise party. Carly seemed rather out of key with the others, but she, presumably, was present as a candidate for their host's bed, rather than as an asset at the dinner table.

Which I can't claim to be either, Katy thought ruefully.

Presently, three of the yacht's eight motor-boats zoomed ashore with a bathing party of crew members, and shortly afterwards Commander Longhurst and Charles came to join the passengers.

The Commander had a slight paunch, but Charles's physique was unchanged since the last time she had seen him in swimming trunks. Thalia, who had been looking rather bored, perked up at the sight of his tall, bronzed figure approaching.

The yacht's owner introduced his officers

to the guests whom they had not met, and Charles fell into conversation with Alain de Noailles until Thalia intervened.

Katy heard her say, "I'm hoping to learn to water-ski on this trip. Are you an expert skier, Charles?"

"I ski — yes. I shouldn't call myself expert."

But you are, Katy thought.

"I'm sure you're being modest," said Thalia. "Would you teach me the rudiments?"

"I should be delighted," he answered, "but someone far better qualified to do that is our Medical Officer, Dr Kent. You haven't met him because he's spending a couple of nights ashore with friends of his parents who live here. He'll be back on board early tomorrow, before we sail, and he's an expert on water-skis. Also, providing everyone continues to enjoy their present good health, his duties are less pressing than mine."

All this was said so agreeably that probably she didn't realise she was being brushed off, and nor would Katy have known it but for his reference, on the bridge, to Thalia's thinness. Katy had forgotten that women did not appeal to him who were too slender, and unrounded in the right places. If anything he preferred a woman who was plump to a bony one, and Thalia's boyish chest would exclude her from being counted attractive by Charles, realised Katy, with relief.

She watched him leave Thalia in conversation with Alain and dive into the pool to surface at the far end, and then come back in her direction with the strong measured strokes which were as pleasing to watch as his lithe, upright stride was on land. She had always liked seeing Charles swim. With flippers, he could surge through the sea at tremendous speed, and even without them he outclassed most men in the water.

I love that man, she thought in an echo of Valentina's phrase. And now I could be a good wife to him, such a good wife — if only he would give me a second chance.

Spyros Dracoulis and his wife did not arrive until an hour before dinner. Katy was in her cabin when she heard a power-boat approaching and looked out of a port to see a man with the same thick, steel-grey hair as her host's sitting in the stern with a blonde who looked not much older than Arianna.

The Greek girl had suggested that they should dress for dinner that night. Probably she had some stunning dress in her wardrobe which she wanted to wear for Alain's benefit.

Having washed and dried her hair, Katy considered what to put on. She had brought with her four evening dresses, and a selection of separates. One of the dresses she had worn on her honeymoon, which they had spent at an hotel in the old, walled city of Peñiscola, used to re-create mediaeval Valencia in the American film starring Charlton Heston in the part of the great Spanish hero, *El Cid.*

The dress was of sea-green chiffon with a bead-scattered bodice. It was not the kind of style which dated and, unable to bring herself to part with it, she had kept it, unworn, in a box until coming on this cruise. She wondered if Charles would recognise it. Probably not. Anyway, it was more suitable for Christmas Eve or Christmas Night. Tonight she would wear a little off-the-peg number, and conserve her dazzle for later on.

Having put up her hair and dressed, she looked at herself in the mirror-clad doors of the cupboards and was not displeased with her reflection. Her white dress was so plain and simple it looked much better than it was. She had discarded the plastic belt which went with it, and substituted a narrow diamanté belt bought long ago in Paris. Then she had turned up the hem to replace an ugly line of machine-stitching with invisible hand-hemming. Her shoes were silver kid T-straps; her bag a slim silver envelope. Liberally scented with *Rive Gauche*, she left her cabin to go and tap on Thalia's door.

Not far from her door was a niche which, earlier, had been filled by a vase of white roses. Now they had been replaced with dark red carnations to which a middle-aged woman in a white silk shirt and pearls with a black skirt was putting the finishing touches.

She turned to smile at Katy, and say, "Good evening, Miss Brown. I am Madame Jourdain, the housekeeper. I hope you find your quarters entirely to your comfort?"

"Most comfortable, thank you, Madame."

On impulse, Katy added, "We are col-leagues. I keep house for Miss Harcourt in London. But my duties are very much less onerous than yours must be, with this huge yacht to run. It's like a mansion, isn't it?"

"It is quite an exacting task to keep everything running smoothly, but I have an excellent staff and I have been doing it for fourteen years," the Frenchwoman replied. "Would it interest you, when you have an hour to spare some time, to see something of our domestic arrangements?"

"I should like nothing better," said Katy eagerly. "But it should be when you can spare the time, Madame. I'm at leisure for ten days, and can easily fit in with your convenience."

A bleeping note, which came from the pocket of Madame's skirt, made her say, "Excuse me, please. I am wanted."

Katy went on her way. She found Thalia still in a wrapper, at work on her evening make-up, which took at least half an hour.

"There's a Doctor Kent, the yacht's M.O., coming on board tomorrow morning. He may do for you," said Thalia, as Katy sat down to wait for her.

"I'm happy just to swim and sunbathe. I don't need any special male companionship."

"Are you missing Robert?" asked the other girl.

Katy shook her head. "You were right — Robert isn't the man for me. I'll have to tell him that as soon as we get back to England."

"You weren't certain before. Now you are. What made up your mind?"

"My own uncertainty, I suppose. What are you wearing tonight?"

Thalia rose from the dressing-stool, and took from her wardrobe a dress of scarlet crêpe-de-chine with a smocked yoke, and a sash to restrain the fullness at the waist. It was a style which only a thin girl could wear successfully. Anyone else would have looked terrible in it.

At dinner, as Katy had expected, the two officers were present. But as she and Charles were on the same side of the table, separated by Taylor and then Marietta, she did not have to restrain herself from looking at him too often. Her other neighbour was Alain who, while

Arianna was chatting to her uncle, seated opposite the young banker, turned and made himself agreeable to Katy.

The Greek girl must have given him a run-down on his fellow guests, as his opening remark was, "I hear you are a keen swimmer, Miss Brown. So am I. Do you ski and scuba?"

"I ski and snorkel I haven't done any scuba diving."

"We must remedy that." Like Andreas, he spoke perfect, idiomatic English with hardly any accent. "Scuba diving is even more enjoyable than snorkelling."

Soon he was calling her Katy. She liked him, and wondered if he and Arianna would marry. With the man on her left, Taylor Stevenson, she talked about solar heating, a subject he raised and which she knew something about, the villa in Spain having had it.

After dinner they were taken to a large games room on the poop deck — air-conditioned like the rest of *Artemis* — which was also a cinema. There they watched a new American film, before returning to the main deck to dance on the pool, now drained and with its bottom raised to deck level.

At an earlier stage in her life, Katy had been to many a lavish party, but never had she seen a more beautiful setting for dancing than the lamplit deck of *Artemis*, surrounded by moon-silvered sea, and with the dark shape of Tobago and its twinkling lights in the background.

With the exception of herself, all the six other women were exquisitely dressed and bejewelled, and looked as beautiful as the butterflies of which, so Alain had said at dinner, there were over six hundred species to be found in Trinidad and Tobago, which was almost double the number in the whole of the United States.

Perhaps because he was aware that she was the only woman present who had no jewels, and who was wearing a cheap dress, Andreas chose her as his first partner. He danced with great vigour and enjoyment, and didn't look foolish while doing it, as sometimes older men did when they took part in modern dancing. When the lively music was followed by something more leisurely, he put his arm round Katy's waist and drew her against him, but not too close.

"What is your impression of Alain?" he asked.

"That he's very nice . . . and in love with your daughter," she answered.

"Yes, I think they may announce their engagement during this cruise. I shall be pleased if they do. He is wealthy in his own right. It is not my money which attracts him, only Arianna herself."

Katy was not unfamiliar with the hazards of being the daughter of a rich man, even though Howard White's income had been a pittance compared with the almost unimaginable riches of the man with whom she was dancing.

He said, "I am thinking of marrying again myself."

Surprised that he should confide this to her, she was startled into saying, "You're going to marry Miss Martin?"

He drew back to look into her eyes with a quizzical glint in his own very dark brown Greek eyes. "Does that strike you as likely?"

"Not very."

"Not at all. Miss Martin would not have me."

You must be joking! She'd jump at you,

was Katy's thought.

"She has no desire to spend the greater part of the next ten years in Valentina's condition," Andreas went on. "It would spoil her figure and interfere with her career to provide me with the sons which are my reason for marrying again. When my daughter was born there were complications which made it inadvisable for Artemis to have any more babies. My second and third wives I married for the pleasure of their beauty. Now I look for a wife who will give me children to inherit my financial empire."

"Is it wise to say so? You could find yourself inundated with volunteers," Katy said lightly.

"That is one of the reasons I live on a ship rather than on land," was his answer. "It makes it easier to escape being pestered by the press and by importunate young ladies who, although they know nothing about me as a man, are prepared to share my bed."

Over his shoulder, Katy caught sight of Charles dancing with Thalia.

Andreas jerked her attention back to him by asking, "Would you be in the queue if

I called for volunteers to become my fourth and last wife, Katy?"

As she looked at him in startled silence, he added, "Don't rebuke me for conceit. I know it's not for my personal charms that many women would welcome me as a husband."

"No, I shouldn't be in the queue."

"Why not, may I ask? Because you don't fancy a husband who, when you are wearing high heels, is half an inch shorter than you are? Don't be afraid to be truthful."

She said, "In bare feet, you're taller than I, and I think you know that, if you weren't a millionaire, you would have no trouble in charming a great many women."

"Yes, I seem to recall having one or two successes before I became a millionaire," he agreed.

"Really? But I thought you married very young, and were probably faithful to your first wife?" she said, since he had encouraged her to be candid.

"I did, and I was. But although Greek girls of my generation were virgins until they were brides, Greek boys were not so restricted. I began making love at fifteen when I was as tall as I am now, and I had the good fortune to meet the first of several older women who were kind enough to teach me the things men should know about women, but which their own husbands didn't. However, that's a digression. I should still like to know why you wouldn't wish to be married to me."

"Because, although my father wasn't a millionaire, he had enough money to indulge all my youthful whims, and it didn't make me happy. As you said this morning, at breakfast, only work and love can do that."

The music ended. As he released her, Andreas asked, "What was your father's business?"

She told him, avoiding going into details by saying, "I'm suddenly very thirsty. Do you think I could have a soft drink, please?"

"Of course." He signalled one of the stewards who were standing discreetly in the background, ready to replenish people's glasses as soon as they were empty. The order given, her host steered her to a chair near Valentina and Taylor Stevenson. When the music began again,

Taylor asked her to dance with him.

If Andreas had given her one or two surprises, her biggest surprise of the evening came about midnight when Charles came to her side just as some slow music was starting.

He had danced at least once with all the other women present, except Valentina who had danced only with her husband and who had now gone to bed, as had Commander Longhurst. But Katy had not expected Charles to be equally dutiful towards her, and probably no one would have noticed if he had avoided a dance with her.

It was a strange sensation, moving into the arms of a man with whom she had once been on terms of the most uninhibited intimacy, and with whom she had now to pretend to be almost a stranger.

Whereas, as Andreas had remarked, her silver sandals made her fractionally taller than him, Charles towered over her, however high her heels. Long ago, at the very beginning of their relationship, he had given her one of his rather wicked smiles and said that to kiss her standing up gave him a crick in his neck: it would be better if she sat on his lap, better still if they were to lie down.

"What time do we sail in the morning?" she asked, as a kind of defence against the sensations aroused by the feel of his arm round her waist and his brown hand enfolding hers.

"Not too early. We try not to disturb the passengers' beauty sleep. Most of them don't have breakfast as early as you and Mr Dracoulis."

So he knew she had been invited into the Owner's private quarters, and probably thought she had engineered it.

"Is one's every move watched?" she asked stiffly.

"Not a great deal escapes the crew's notice."

"Clearly. But I'm rather surprised that the First Officer should listen to gossip among the stewards."

"The First Officer doesn't," Charles said levelly. "But the Captain's tiger keeps him in touch with all that goes on in the crew's quarters, and the Captain mentions some things to his second in command. When the passenger list includes several contenders for the dogaressa's bed, the crew spend a lot of time discussing the odds. The Owner sleeps in a bed which is said to have belonged to the wife of a doge when Venice was a republic — as you may see for yourself before Christmas is over," he added sardonically.

Katy was determined not to let him enrage her a second time. She said coolly, "It's a good thing you're backing Miss Martin. If you put your money on me, you'd lose it. And it may interest you to know that Mr Dracoulis, who must be no mean judge of people, has formed quite a different opinion of my morals from your uncharitable reading of them. In fact he warned me — and suggested I should warn Thalia — that although he would trust you with his life, our virtue might not be too safe with you. He described you as being 'something of a pirate where women are concerned'. But of course I already knew that."

His arm closed more firmly around her; his grip on her other hand tightened. "What the devil do you mean by that remark?"

"It's hardly the act of an officer and gentleman to seduce a girl. Admittedly you did make an honest woman of me afterwards, but even so . . . "

She had spoken lightly and teasingly, only wanting to remind him that, although she had had many shortcomings when he had known her before, she had never been a promiscuous girl. He had been her first and, even if he would not believe it, her only lover. But he did know he had been first with her. That fact was incontrovertible.

But her indignation was refuelled when his answer was, "It wasn't hard to seduce you, was it? Would Dracoulis find it any harder than I did? I don't think so somehow."

Forgetting who might be watching, she strained away from the sinewy grip on her waist. "You have no right to say that, Charles! Because, at nineteen, I didn't hold out against the man I loved, it doesn't mean I must be a light woman now."

"Most women are light women with Dracoulis."

"Perhaps. I don't happen to be one of them."

"You haven't been put to the test yet."

She was still pulling back on his arm,

disliking their physical contact while his eyes held so much contempt. Suddenly, with a faint, cruel smile twisting his mouth, he drew her hard against his chest, and she felt his long muscular thighs against hers. For a moment she tried to resist, but not only was it physically impossible but, almost at once, the will to resist had died in her. She felt herself melting against him, as she had so often in the old days, her whole body beginning to tremble with the half-forgotten excitement of feeling fragile and helpless in the arms of a tall, strong man whose shoulder, under her hand, felt as solid and strong as rock. Robert had not fully revived the feeling. Charles did, immediately.

"Please, Charles . . . don't," she protested softly.

"You used to like it," he murmured mockingly.

"You used to love me. Now you seem to hate and despise me."

The music was almost at an end. While the last bars were playing he continued to hold her close, not replying to her last remark. At the very end, a few seconds before he had to release her, she became aware that, although she might never reanimate his affection, she could still arouse his desire. She found herself blushing like the inexperienced girl she had been when he met her. As they drew apart, his expression was closed and inscrutable.

"Thank you," he said, with a slight bow, taking her lightly by the elbow to walk her back to the chair where she had been sitting.

Marietta Dracoulis came to talk to her. She was French and not, as Katy had thought on first glimpsing her, many years younger than her husband. It was an illusion caused by the girlish slimness of her figure and the blondeness of her beautifully dyed hair. Seen at close quarters, she was only a year or two younger than Spyros, who looked to be about fifty, a few years older than his brother.

About a quarter of an hour later the departure of the Stevensons to their cabin gave Katy a cue to make her escape. Always, when in hot climates, she had slept in her skin, a nightdress somewhere at hand in case of emergency. Her last act before climbing into bed was to remove the tiny pearl ear-studs which Charles had given her as a wedding present, but the delicate chain which went with them she left round her neck, night and day, only noticing that it was there when she looked at herself in the mirror. It had become as much part of her as her wedding ring had once been, until she had taken it off and put it away in a safe place. He had not given her an engagement ring because there had been no engagement. Their love for each other acknowledged, the next step had been to get married.

On this second night on board *Artemis*, although the day and the evening had not been lacking in trauma, she made an effort to read when she was in bed.

The sheet drawn up to her armpits, a glass of water at her elbow, she began *At One With The Sea* by Naomi James, the intrepid young New Zealand woman who, newly married and with only two years' sailing experience, had made sailing history.

Remembering the first few months of her marriage to Charles, Katy could imagine no circumstances in which she would have left him for long, and she was very curious to discover the motives which had spurred the young and attractive helmswoman to desert her bridegroom.

Nevertheless, in spite of her interest in the book, she found it hard to concentrate on it. Thoughts of Charles would keep intervening. How could she convince him she had no designs on Andreas?

She had been striving to read for about twenty minutes when to her astonishment, the door opened and Charles himself appeared.

Taken aback, she said, "What do you want?"

"What do you think I want, Katy?"

His grey eyes were curiously brilliant, as if he had had too much to drink, except that Charles never drank too much — or never had in her time with him.

"I — I don't know," she stammered, closing the book.

"Earlier today you asked me if there was anything left between us but enmity. On my side there is one thing left. I still find you extremely bedworthy."

"Charles, it's very late . . . " she began.

"Are you nervous, Katy?" he mocked her. "You were never timid before, not

110

even when I seduced you, as you put it."

He turned, and she heard the key turn in the lock. Then he took off his hat and sent it spinning towards the chair where Thalia had sat the night before, discussing her appetite for him.

"As I recall, you were only too willing to learn about love," he said, coming towards where she lay. "And by now, no doubt, you can teach me a thing or two."

Sitting down on the side of the bed, he removed the book from her lap and put it aside on the night table. His hand reached out towards the top of the sheet. "You've no need to be shy with me, Katy. I'm your husband, remember? And even if I were not, your breasts are — or were, when last I saw them — in no way inferior to those which Miss Martin displays for our delectation."

Katy fended his hand, and clutched the sheet more tightly round her. Beginning to tremble, she said, "You're tight, Charles. Please go away."

"On the contrary, I am cold sober."

"You are not going to make love to me,"

Katy said sharply, but with a quaver in her voice.

"You think not?" He smiled, but his eyes were not amused. They were merciless. "I think I shall do whatever I please with you," he told her.

3

"CHARLES – no! You've no right," she begged, shrinking.

For answer he bent towards her and kissed her hard on the mouth. At first she kept her lips closed, twisting her head from side to side in an effort to escape the relentless pressure of his lips.

His arms were on either side of her, gripping the bedhead. Her slim hands, balled into fists, were beating him off, and having as little effect as a child in a tantrum vainly pounding its parent.

Had he been a stranger, bent on rape, she would have fought him tooth and nail. But how could she bite and scratch a man in whose arms she had known only exquisite pleasure? Although it was so long ago that she felt sure that, if he took her, it would be scarcely less painful than her first initiation.

She felt her mouth start to soften, and gave up her frantic pounding of his muscle-armoured chest and shoulders. Slowly her

113

arm crept round him as she accepted his kisses, her body beginning to relax.

His hands left the bedhead and shifted her lower on the pillows until she was flat on her back and he was stretched out beside her. Unresisting, she let him draw the sheet down from her armpits to her waist and begin to caress her. Her eyes shut, she closed her mind to everything but the pleasure of the moment.

This was how it had been on the sloop, the first time he had made love to her. She had not drunk wine in those days, only Coke, so it had not been wine which had made her an easy conquest, only love; her own love for Charles, and the heart-aching need to be loved of a girl who had never before felt close to anyone. Although Howard White had given her everything she wanted, he had never given her affection, having none to give.

Now, all over again, while Charles's mouth sealed hers in kiss after long, scorching kiss, and his hand roamed over the soft skin which he had uncovered, she re-lived the emotional struggle of her first unforgettable surrender to him.

As before she was torn between wanting

114

to give in completely, and the feeling that it would be wrong. The reason was different this time, but equally powerful. Then she had been a virgin, giving herself to a man who might not value her gift, and had not yet said they had a future together. Now she was his wife, and love was no longer a mystery; but was this love flaming between them, or only a hot burst of lust of which, later, she would feel ashamed?

As Charles's hand slid under the sheet, stroking her stomach, rediscovering her hips and thighs, Katy shuddered and gave a low moan of mingled delight and indecision. It had been so long since she had felt the blissful sensations induced by his hot, hungry mouth and slow-moving hand. Must she make him stop? Could she even?

In her heart she knew that she could. He had overpowered her at the beginning, forcing those first ravenous kisses on her whether she liked it or not. But he would not possess her by force. Before he invaded her body, she would be willing and eager, and any pain she might feel after four years of nun-like chastity would have nothing to do with brutality.

"Oh, don't . . . don't," she whispered desperately, as he freed her lips to kiss her throat and her shoulders, each kiss inching lower and lower to where her smooth skin paled a shade from the deeper tone achieved in the past two days to the lighter all-over gold acquired in the solarium in London.

Charles ignored her appeal, as well he might since her words were not matched by the movements of her hands on his shoulders and in his thick hair.

Whether she could, even then, have made herself resist him, she did not find out. A tap at the door made him cease his assault on her senses. He raised his head, and his hand stopped its insidious stroking of her tightly clenched thighs, giving her time to recover a little.

"It must be Thalia," she breathed, as the tapping was repeated.

His face was turned to the door and she could not see his expression. Suddenly he sprang off the bed, snatched his hat off the chair where he had flung it, and disappeared into her bathroom, shutting the door quietly behind him.

Surely he can't imagine that I'm going to

let Thalia in, with lovemaking written all over me? Katy thought, stifling a slightly hysterical laugh.

Knowing the cabin door was sufficiently thick and well made to make it impossible for anyone standing outside to hear soft sounds from within, she hoisted herself into a sitting position and reached behind her to straighten her disordered pillows before pulling up the crumpled sheet and tucking it round her, as it had been when Charles entered. How long ago? Five minutes? It seemed much, much longer.

Her pulse had not yet resumed its normal unnoticeable beat. Her skin was still tingling with the desire he had aroused in her. But the thought of Thalia's reaction, had she seen him coming into this cabin, had a very sobering effect on her. Thalia would have been furious, and not unreasonably. If she didn't suspect Katy of deliberately filching the man she wanted for herself, she would be piqued that he preferred someone else.

Several times in the past two years, Katy had seen Thalia angry. The anger had never been directed at her, but at people in the designer's professional life.

But those episodes had made the younger girl hope that she never would incur her employer's wrath, for Thalia enraged was a very different person from Thalia in a good mood.

I should have told her Charles was my estranged husband, Katy thought uneasily.

If it had been Thalia outside, she did not knock a third time, and presently Charles emerged from the bathroom, his expression very different from that with which he had entered the cabin. His grey eyes no longer held the fierce, dangerous gleam which had, for a few minutes, frightened her. Now they looked merely grim, as they had so often in the past when his marriage had been turning sour.

He said quietly, "I'll be at the pool at sunrise. Be there."

A moment later he was gone, leaving her to wrestle with the longings he had kindled but not satisfied, and with the problem of whether they had any hope of being reconciled still unresolved.

It was five minutes past sunrise and the eastern sky was ablaze with rose and gold streaks when Katy, wrapped in the white

118

robe, arrived at the pool and saw Charles's tall figure by the ship's rails.

Although she moved almost silently over the deck, he heard her coming and turned when she was two yards from him.

"Good morning," she said, in a low voice, remaining where she was and resting her arms on the polished dark wood of the top rail.

He reduced the distance between them to a yard. "Good morning." There was a pause before he said, "I'm not going to apologise for what happened in your cabin last night. Contrary to the impression given you by Dracoulis, nowadays I keep my relations with women to a minimum. Being a normal male, I can't do without them completely. It's unfortunate that you have appeared on the scene after a rather long interval in that side of my life. It was a mistake to dance with you. Having said that, I can't guarantee that it won't happen again. You always had a powerful effect on me."

"And you on me, Charles. At least in that sphere our marriage was a success."

"But in no other," he said coldly. "And although an unsatisfactory sexual relationship may destroy a marriage, a good one is

119

not, on its own, enough to sustain one."

"But it wasn't the only thing between us. We had many more things in common — books, music, the sea. If I'd been more domesticated — "

He interrupted her, a note of impatience in his voice. "Decorative women rarely are, and if they're decorative enough, they don't need to be. They can find themselves husbands who can afford to relieve them of tedious chores."

Katy realised suddenly that because, when Andreas had introduced them, he had spoken of her as Thalia's friend, Charles might still be unaware — unless Thalia had mentioned it to him, which seemed unlikely — that his wife, since their separation, had become extremely domesticated.

She was about to tell him so, when he went on, "I should like you to know that as soon as I heard about your father, which wasn't till months after his death because I was in the Pacific and never saw any English newspapers, I made every effort to trace you and offer my help."

"Did you? I'm glad of that, Charles. It did hurt me, during the trial, to think that you might be in Europe and not want to know. I daresay it didn't come as much of a shock to you — Father's trial and imprisonment, I mean. You never liked him, did you?"

"I always suspected that his activities were not altogether above board. That's one of the reasons I wouldn't accept the post he offered me. Had I trusted him, I might have done."

"You didn't tell me that."

"There were enough rifts between us without my impugning your father's honesty on no better evidence than a hunch. You would have been angry and defensive, and we should have quarrelled yet again."

"Yes, I suppose you're right. But all that's a long time ago. Need we go on quarrelling, Charles?"

He took some time to answer, his brooding gaze fixed on the horizon. At length, he said, "No, I suppose not. We can strive to be 'civilised', as they say."

"You don't think we might . . . try again?"

His eyebrows shot up. "You're joking!"

"Is it such a crazy suggestion?"

"I shouldn't describe it as sensible," he said, in his dryest tone. "You're allowing what happened last night to cloud your judgment. You want me as a lover, not as a husband. If we spent a few nights together you'd soon realise it was only the old powerful sex urge at work."

She saw his eyes narrow a little and, after a pause, he went on, "Not that I'm unwilling to accommodate you. Yes, why not indeed? Unsatisfied urges play hell with one's concentration. If we both want each other, why shouldn't we get it out of our system? Of course it could queer your pitch with Dracoulis. I don't think he'd like being pre-empted by one of his officers . . . if he found out. He might not. Not everything filters back to him."

The glint which had been in his eyes when he came to her cabin the night before had rekindled while he was speaking. He reached out his hand to touch her.

She struck it away and said furiously, "How dare you speak to me like that! I've told you before, I'm not here for that reason. What makes you think in four years I've become a woman who sells herself?"

"Don't take me for a fool, Katy. All your father's assets were confiscated by the tax authorities — I made it my business to look up the full press coverage. You weren't a career girl who could support herself comfortably. And yet here you are, four years later, looking like a million dollars, and associating with a woman who, within an hour of meeting me, had made it clear that, had I gone to *her* cabin the night before last, I'd have been made welcome."

"You said yesterday I had a 'misleadingly innocent look'. I suppose you would never believe that the last man I lay on a bed with was yourself? — and I don't mean last night."

"No, frankly I shouldn't," he answered. "Perhaps you've forgotten those times when I came to your room, after you'd gone back to your father, and we spent half the night making love. You were no nervous virgin by then, my girl. You were hot stuff — very hot stuff. No girl as hot-blooded as you were could live without sex for four years."

"Oh!" she gasped, enraged that the man who had been the first to awaken her, and had taught her everything she knew, should know so little about her. "I didn't realise that what we did was only sex. I thought it was love — quite a different thing. And for love people wait a lifetime. But it seems now I never had it." Her voice broke. She turned away, her eyes blurred by angry tears.

"Katy!" He came up behind her and took her by the shoulders, his grip biting into her flesh.

"Let me go!" She wrenched herself free, and whirled to face him, her cheeks hot with angry humiliation at having her tentative olive branch rejected in such a brutal way.

"You're so right," she told him furiously. "It was crazy to think there was something special between us. I suppose it was just that, like you, I haven't had a lover for some time and, as you so rightly say, I've always been an enthusiast in the bedroom. But don't try my door again, Charles, because you'll find it locked. If it's unlocked, I shan't be there. I'll be in the dogaressa's bed."

On which irately reckless parting shot, she turned on her heel and hurried back to her cabin.

The tears which she shed that morning, lying sprawled face down on the bed where the night before, but for the interruption, she might have let Charles make love to her, were some of the bitterest she had shed in all the long years between their parting and meeting.

Later, drained of tears, she lay in a trance of misery, wishing there was some way for her to extricate herself from the intolerable strain of spending Christmas in a milieu to which she did not belong, under the contemptuous scrutiny of a man to whom she still belonged legally, but in no other way. However, as it was not possible to employ the time-honoured device of sending herself an urgent summons, she would just have to stick it out, she thought, as she pulled herself upright and shook back her tumbled hair.

A hot shower, followed by a cold one, her face uplifted to receive the full impact of the water, did much to restore her physically, and sun-glasses would conceal any lingering trace of puffiness round her eyes.

"You're up late this morning," was Thalia's greeting, when Katy returned to the pool and found several of the others there. "I knocked on your door last night, but you must have been asleep."

"I'm sorry. Was it anything important you wanted?" Katy asked.

"No, no — I only came by for a chat."

"It must be the sea air which is making me sleep more." Katy turned away because Arianna was waiting to introduce a young man who had risen to his feet at her approach.

"This is David Kent, our doctor. David . . . Katy Brown," said Arianna.

They shook hands. He was of medium height with a plain but good-humoured face, and the bright red hair and light blue eyes which were usually accompanied, in hot weather, by a lobster-pink skin. However, if Dr Kent had been through that unbecoming stage at some time, it was long ago. He was now as brown as the rest of the crew, although with a lighter tan than Charles's deep burnished mahogany colouring.

He, Katy was relieved to notice, was not among those present. No doubt he was on the bridge as *Artemis* was now in motion, spreading a wide wake across the dark blue of the deep water her displacement required.

At first sight, Katy was disappointed by Dr Kent whom she had hoped might rival Charles for Thalia's attention. But she knew the other girl too well to suppose that he would appeal to her, although what he lacked in looks he made up for in lively wit.

"The doctor is very amusing, isn't he?" she remarked to Thalia, later on.

"Yes, he is — but not my type," said the designer. "I've never found freckled men sexy, and he's one big freckle."

That afternoon, Madame Jourdain took Katy on a tour behind the scenes of her domain, showing her the pantry galley where Continental breakfasts and other tray snacks were prepared; the ladies' maid's ironing room; the laundry with its washing machine and steam presser; and the enormous walk-in linen stores, one for the crew's plain white linen, and another for the expensive sets of bed linen and towels used in the passengers' cabins.

Another large cupboard was ranged with every good brand of soap, talc, bath salts and other toiletries; and, as in the best hotels, guests were provided with writing paper and envelopes, any letters they wrote being stamped for them by the steward in charge of outgoing mail.

In the galley, which was not her province, but which she thought Katy would like to see, the housekeeper introduced her to one of the three chefs who between them supervised the cooking of the elaborate menus enjoyed by the passengers, and the plainer but very good fare served to the crew.

The tour ended in Madame Jourdain's private sitting-room where, over tea and delicious little cakes, she explained how early widowhood had led her into professional housekeeping from which she was due to retire at the end of the year.

She was telling Katy her retirement plans when someone knocked on the door, and she broke off to call, "Come in."

Katy had not expected to have to face Charles before the evening, and she could not hide her dismay when the door opened and in he walked.

His reaction was one of surprise, and almost instantly he said to the housekeeper,

"I'm sorry to have disturbed you. I'll look in later."

"No, no — come in, please. You aren't disturbing us. Have some tea." She beckoned him to a chair and said to Katy, "Mr Ormond and I sometimes play chess at this hour." To Charles, she said, "I have been showing Miss Brown the parts of the ship under my command, and we have been watching Chef Mario making one of his fleets of meringue swans for dinner tonight. The deftness and speed with which he pipes them never ceases to fascinate me, but of course you have probably never seen him making them."

"No, I haven't," he agreed.

"And you haven't a sweet tooth, have you?" recalled Madame Jourdain. "Such confections are rather wasted on you. I like both to cook and eat sweet things, but you are in accord with Miss Brown who tells me that her specialities are French country soups and *râgouts*. She is Cordon Bleu trained, as I am."

"Is she indeed?" Charles raised an eyebrow, his expression sceptical, although perhaps Madame Jourdain did not recognise it as such.

Unaware of the tension between them, she went on, "Do sit down, Mr Ormond. You seem a giant in this cabin."

"No, I won't intrude on your women's talk. Some other time." He withdrew.

"He's such a nice man, Mr Ormond," said Madame, after the door closed. "But he seems not to like feminine society, except that of women of my age or older."

"Really? But Mr Dracoulis warned us that Mr Ormond was rather a devil with women."

"Only with women of the type whose manners and morals are such that they forfeit respect. With nice women he is always a perfect gentleman, although he avoids the company of the younger ones unless it is part of his social duty. He had an unhappy marriage — not his fault, I feel sure — and it's made him a misogynist. Which is just as well, in a way, because if he were still married he could not have his wife on board. The Captain has been a widower for several years now, but he is the only officer who could — and did — have his wife with him."

For dinner that night Katy wore an

apricot blouse bought at a thrift shop, and a coral and apricot skirt she had run up herself — a combination which Charles would probably assume had cost as much as the outfits worn by the other women.

By now her eyes showed no trace of the tears which had flooded them earlier, and she had begun to regret allowing him to make her lose her temper — and especially to regret that heated and untrue parting shot.

Andreas had not been seen all day. When he joined his guests for drinks before dinner, he apologised for neglecting them but explained that a union dispute on the other side of the Atlantic had necessitated a prolonged exchange of signals with his staff on the spot.

In view of their row that morning, it was discomfiting to find that tonight she was seated between her husband and Janus, although for the first part of the meal the film director conversed with her, and Charles talked to Marietta.

Inevitably the moment came when they were forced to talk to each other, and Charles's opening remark was, "Have you

131

really learned to cook, or were you pulling Madame Jourdain's leg?"

"Why should I do that?"

"I can't imagine, but neither can I imagine you producing a soup which didn't come out of a tin or a packet."

In a lowered voice, she replied, "The last time we met probably you were not capable of fulfilling your present duties."

"True: but I did have a yachtmaster's ticket, and had been in the Navy. You were the most unlikely candidate for a Cordon Bleu diploma one could expect to meet."

She put on a bright social smile. "Life is full of unlikelihood, isn't it?" A slight pause. "Madame Jourdain says you are *so* nice . . . a perfect gentleman."

For the first time since they had met again, she saw in his eyes the flash of amusement which once had been characteristic of him.

"Did you disillusion her?" he asked.

"Naturally not. As you yourself told me yesterday, that could only complicate both our lives."

"On whom do you practise your culinary arts? Your boy-friends?"

She could tell from his tone that he was

still not wholly convinced that the claim made on her behalf by Madame Jourdain was true.

"My employer. I'm a working girl now."

"With excellent holidays, one gathers. Ten days off at Christmas. Exceptionally generous."

The note of sarcasm riled her, but she was determined to keep cool. "My employer is away for Christmas. If you don't believe me, why not ask her — after dinner? I work for Thalia who does a lot of entertaining. I quite regularly cook for a dinner party of this size. Unbelievable, isn't it?"

As, just at that moment, there was a pause in the conversation between Janus and his other neighbour, she turned away from Charles and, disregarding good form, did not speak to him again.

The swans which she had seen in the making earlier were brought in on a dark green glass tray, their fragile sugar wings filled with whipped cream, fresh fruit and nuts. Charles did not have one, she noticed. It had not taken the Frenchwoman's remark to remind her that he had no liking for sweet things.

She retained a clear memory of all his likes and dislikes.

Often, since their estrangement, she had suddenly had a painfully vivid recollection of one of their happy times. She had another when the swans were followed by the cheese board. As two stewards moved round the table and the guests made their choice from a selection of the finest European cheeses, she remembered the many days when she and Charles had lunched in the cockpit of the sloop, sharing a long crusty loaf which he would split with his clasp knife and pack with slices of salami, onion and tomato. Sometimes the filling would be a white cheese from the market, liberally dusted with black pepper. Always there would be a bottle of wine to share and, more often than not, afterwards they would go below and make love before swimming again. That had been before it had been necessary to take to chartering for a living, after which there had been no privacy during the day, and no more peaceful bread and cheese lunches à *deux*. Did Charles have similar memories? Did he ever share her regret, she wondered, as she cut herself some *bleu d'Auvergne* and, when the cheese board moved on, covertly watched him selecting his favourite Camembert.

After dinner there was another film show and, later, dancing. By now the yacht was lying at anchor off a small uninhabited island.

At midnight their ebullient host suggested moonlight bathing from the island's beach. Everyone, including Valentina, went below to change into swimsuits and beach wraps. Very soon they were all ashore, drinking yet more champagne on sand almost as fine as talcum powder and still warm from the day's sun.

Some of the party did not swim but launched themselves off from the shallows in transparent inflated armchairs, like enormous bubbles. In these, beating their feet and whipping up cascades of foam, they propelled themselves about.

Katy walked into the sea until she was up to her waist in water as clear as gin and as warm as a tepid bath. Then she struck out, her long hair loose. When she stopped in deep water to turn on her back and float, the voices and laughter of the others came to her across the surface, but she had a curious sensation of isolation and unreality, as if she were watching another movie, not taking part in an actual event.

She saw someone swimming towards her, and recognised Charles's unhurried, almost splashless strokes. A yard away he trod water, lifting a glistening arm — Red Indian dark in the moonlight — to rake back his wet black hair.

"I've been detailed to shepherd you back to the flock. Your host doesn't know you're more at home in the water than some of the female contingent."

Katy felt sure that he hadn't been sent to fetch her back. She had been listening and watching. Voices carried so clearly across water that she would have heard Andreas speak to him. And the Greek had seen her swimming and knew she was not a one-foot-on-the-bottom bather like Paulette and Thalia. Charles had followed her of his own accord, even if he didn't wish to admit it.

"Very well." She began to swim back, but with the most leisurely of breast strokes, keeping her head out of the water.

When he followed suit, it confirmed that

he wanted to talk to her.

"So you really are Thalia's cook — and very good, so she tells me," he said, after four or five strokes.

"I couldn't see myself in an office job, and I had to do something. You can take some of the credit for my success, Charles. It was all your nasty remarks which spurred me to prove that anything you could do — in the galley — I could do at least as well and, by now, rather better. If you're ever in London, looking up Thalia, perhaps I shall have the chance to prove it to you."

"Perhaps."

"Are your leaves as generous as mine?" she asked, unable to resist reminding him of his sarcastic comment during dinner.

"They depend on the Owner's movements. We have a minimum annual leave, and sometimes considerably more if *Artemis* is not in use."

It had not escaped her notice that instead of returning to the others, he was swimming at a slight angle which would bring them ashore some distance away from the little heaps on the sand which were discarded bathing wraps, and the steward in charge of the champagne.

"Where do you go on your leave?"

"To Fontainebleau, usually."

"Why there?"

"One of my aunts married a Frenchman. They lived there. He died before her and, having no children, she left their house to me. It's let, but I have a small flat on the top floor. I've always liked France, and it's convenient for Paris or the country, as the mood takes me."

They swam on in silence until Katy's feet touched sand and she stood up. In a low voice which wouldn't carry, she said, "Charles . . . what I said to you this morning wasn't true. You made me angry, and I — I said something I didn't mean."

"You said a number of things. Which one are you thinking of?"

"About the . . . the dogaressa's bed. I shall never sleep in it. That was just an outburst of anger because you would persist in misjudging me."

"But you meant what you said about locking your door against me?"

She hesitated. "Yes . . . yes, I did mean that, because it could only be painful for

138

us to have that sort of affair. Believe it or not, as you like, but I never have had one, and I'm not going to start now — even with you."

But even as she spoke, she was sharply aware of his tall, strong, sinewy body, and of her own deep-seated longing to be held in those powerful arms, her softness pressed to his hardness. The emotions aroused last night were still very close to the surface.

"What held you back? You're a beautiful girl and, as you recently reminded me, the double standard has given place to equality."

"For unmarried people — yes. I'm not unmarried, unless now you're prepared to give me my freedom."

"Have you any particular reason for wanting your freedom?"

As he spoke, his gaze left her face and travelled slowly, caressingly downwards. She was wearing a tan-coloured bikini, the top dependent on a single length of cotton rope which circled her back and was threaded through the base of the two small triangles of fabric before V-ing upwards and outwards in a loop which tied at the nape of her neck. The bottom front and back triangles, equally scanty, were held by another piece of rope which knotted on her left hip.

"In this light, in that thing, you look naked," he said huskily, making her realise that he, too — perhaps more than she — was still in the grip of the passion they had generated the night before.

Had they belonged to a different, more primitive culture, he would have picked her up and carried her to the dark shadows under the trees, there to give rein to all the pent-up desire which was throbbing inside them.

He was thinking the same thing. He said, "If we were islanders in the Pacific — "

"But we aren't," she interrupted hastily. "And the others" — she was thinking of Thalia — "may be wondering why we're standing here by ourselves instead of joining in the party."

Turning, she waded ashore and walked along the wet sand at the edge of the water to where she had left her towel and wrap. When she glanced back, Charles had gone into the sea again, and was swimming as if there were a shark at his heels. Or like a man trying to work something out of his system, she thought, hoping the same thought would not strike anyone else who might have noticed their short tête-à-tête.

Bowls of hot consommé were awaiting the party when they returned on board, and light snacks for those who felt the night was still young.

Drawing Katy aside, Andreas asked, "Would you care to join me for breakfast?"

"Thank you, but I don't think I shall be rising as early as you do tomorrow. I need my eight hours, especially at sea."

"Another day, perhaps."

"Perhaps."

It was two o'clock in the morning before she was able to climb into bed, having had to rinse and dry her hair. Probably for midnight bathes it was better to wear a cap as some of the other women had. But she had never worn a bathing cap, and felt that even a bikini was really an encumbrance in the water. Perhaps one night she would set the alarm buzzer of the bedside clock to wake her up at an hour when no one else was about, and then creep quietly down the accommodation ladder to have a swim in her skin.

Although she did not really expect Charles to repeat his visit of the night before, she had turned the key in her lock after entering the cabin.

But, as she was sitting up in bed, smoothing some cream into her hands before switching off the light, she saw the door handle moving and knew it could only be him, putting her statement to the test. Her heart gave a nervous lurch. Thank heavens she had remembered to turn the key! Since locking her door was not a habit, she might easily have neglected to do so and, in consequence, been subjected to a repetition of last night's ordeal.

Ordeal? an inner voice seemed to murmur derisively. When was being in bed with Charles ever an ordeal? It was always bliss and, when you get back to your nun-like life in London — because you definitely can't go on seeing Robert after this — you'll regret all these foolish scruples. You want Charles. He wants you. Life is short, and often unhappy. Take all the pleasures it offers.

Yes, that's all very well, but before, whenever he made love to me, his mind was involved . . . his heart, Katy argued with herself. Now I don't know what he feels about me. Not hate, perhaps — but not love.

Next day she was not surprised when, before lunch, Thalia came to her cabin to chat and after some conversation, asked, "What were you and Charles discussing while you were standing in the shallows with him during the beach party last night?"

"He was telling me about a house in France which an aunt left him when she died. I gather he spends his leaves there. It's at Fontainebleau — very convenient for a gay whirl in Paris, or quieter pursuits in the country. I should think it's a splendid investment, too. Have you been to Fontainebleau, Thalia? It's a most attractive little town, although I suppose it must become horribly crowded with tourists visiting the palace during the season."

Katy hoped she sounded as casual as if she were reporting the gist of a conversation she had had with Janus or Taylor.

"Did he mention his wife?" Thalia asked.

"Why should he mention her to me?"

"He might have. People do confide in you."

"Only laundrymen and old ladies at bus-stops. Not people like the First Officer," said Katy, using his rank rather than his name to make it sound as if, to her, he was merely one of the ship's officers in whom she had no special interest.

Thalia, having stubbed out one cigarette, put her lighter to the tip of another. "I don't seem to be getting far with him, and who else is there?" she said petulantly. "Janus is a doting husband. Taylor isn't, I fancy, but he doesn't switch me on, nor does the doctor. The Captain is too old. Andreas is too short, and Alain, who *is* my type, is all too clearly out of bounds. So that leaves only Charles, who makes himself very agreeable up to a point but no further."

"It's a pity you brought me with you. You could have brought your own man."

"Didn't have one to bring except Philip, and I'm tired of him," was Thalia's reply. "It seemed reasonable to assume there would be a choice of men here."

"I'm surprised you don't find Andreas attractive."

"My taste runs to six-footers, but the only one available is taking so long to make a move that I'm not sure he's going to. And when I'm not working I have a lot of surplus energy."

It was a subject which Katy would have liked to drop, but she knew that this was only because it involved Charles. Had Dr Kent been the one whom Thalia had her eye on, the rôle of her confidante would have been much less uncomfortable.

She said, "When I was having tea with Madame Jourdain, the housekeeper, yesterday afternoon, the First Officer came in for a moment or two. He plays chess with her sometimes, but when he saw me there he went away. She mentioned that he had been known to get involved with passengers, but only with the obviously easy ones. He doesn't make passes at nice women."

"And he thinks I'm nice?" said Thalia, with a yelp of laughter. "I've got news for him. I'm far from nice. Maybe I'd better make it plainer," she decided, in a more cheerful tone. She got up to go. "See you at lunch."

She left Katy feeling very uneasy. After

pacing her cabin for some minutes, she lifted the receiver of her telephone and, when a male voice said, "Switchboard," asked if she could be put through to the First Officer.

"Certainly, madam. One moment, please."

Although she had not given her name, no doubt the operator could tell from which cabin the request had come. Would he listen in? Would he gossip? In case he did, and it reached the ears of the Owner, she would have to think of an innocuous explanation.

"First Officer speaking."

Although she had been waiting for it, Charles's deep, resonant voice made her start.

"I — I'm sorry to bother you, but could I have a word with you . . . in private."

Afterwards she wondered if he recognised her voice, or if the operator had already told him who was calling him.

He said, "Certainly. Shall I come to your cabin?"

"Oh, no — no, please don't do that. Could I come to yours?"

He gave the necessary directions. "I'll be there in five minutes." She heard a click as he replaced his receiver.

Nobody saw her enter his cabin, and close the door with a sigh of relief at being unobserved. If she could get away unseen, and the switchboard operator was a discreet man, it might be that only he would ever know she had been here.

Charles's quarters were not as spacious as hers, but nevertheless they were comfortably furnished and attractively decorated in an appropriately masculine style. An inner door suggested that he had a private bathroom or, more probably, a shower.

Books, some of which she recognised, filled recessed shelves within arm's reach of the single berth with its tailored cover. Otherwise no personal belongings were visible unless the two antique charts on the bulkheads belonged to him. They might be part of the décor.

It seemed a long time before he joined her, and she began to wonder if she had been foolish to come. At last the door opened. Charles entered, closed the door and hung his hat on a peg on the back of it.

Then, before she could start to explain why she had sought a private talk with him, he crossed the short space between them and took her firmly in his arms. Her exclamation of surprise and protest became a smothered murmur as his mouth closed warmly over hers.

Had it been the first time he had kissed her on *Artemis*, she would have fought him off. But, as they had been last night on the moonlit beach, her responses were still easily excited. He had only to crush her against him, and she was in the same heady state in which he had left her lying on the bed in her cabin while he disappeared into the bathroom.

Before she knew what she was doing, she had opened her lips and slid her arms round his waist, clinging to him as ardently as he was holding her.

He kissed her like a survivor of the desert slaking a thirst which had driven him almost to madness; and she, too, wanted never to stop being strained almost painfully tight, her head bent back in ecstatic submission.

At last he loosened his hold, but only to step back enough to begin unbuttoning the shirt she had put on for lunch.

"Couldn't you wait until after lunch, when our absence wouldn't have been noticed?" he asked, with a teasing glint.

Dazed by the onslaught of his kiss, she pushed feebly at his hands, her own hands trembling.

"Charles, I didn't come here for this. Please stop . . . *please!*" she implored.

"What? *Oh, God!*" With a deep groan he swung away from her, clenching his fists and pounding them against the bulkhead where he held them, his tall head bent, every line of his back indicative of tension and frustration.

She knew better than to touch him or even to speak until he had regained control of the powerful urge which was an ache inside her, and which must be agony for him.

At length, without moving, he asked, "What did you come for?"

"To ask your advice . . . your help. Above all, to beg you not to come to my cabin as I think you did again last night."

Slowly he straightened and turned to face her, his lean brown face taut with strain.

She wanted to hold out her arms, to say,

"Oh, my love, if you want me, take me." But she held her tongue, waiting for him to lash her with sarcasm. This time she felt she deserved it for not stopping to think of the construction he might have put — had put — on her request to see him privately.

But when Charles spoke, his tone was weary rather than caustic. "Yes, I came," he agreed. "I don't know what it is about you, Katy. I've met women equally beautiful who didn't have any effect on me. But you're like a drug . . . an aphrodisiac. I married you knowing it was a damn stupid thing to do, but unable to stop myself. Now it's started all over again. If it were merely that I needed a woman, I could work it off with your man-eating friend Thalia Harcourt. But it isn't just that. I want you."

"But only temporarily, in your bed. Not in your life."

"There isn't a place for a woman in my life now. I like my job, I've no intention of giving it up. I've told you, I want you like hell, and every day you're on board will be more of a strain. But you won't be on board indefinitely, and after you've gone back to

London I shall get you out of my system as I did before — as one can overcome any addiction if the cigarettes, or the alcohol, or the woman aren't there to tempt one. In the meantime, as you obviously want me — in spite of your protests — I may yet find my way into bed with you."

She shook her head. "No, you won't, Charles. If there was a place in your life for me, I believe I could make you much happier than I ever did four years ago. But sex, for me, is part of love, and love is total commitment — mind, body and soul, now and always. Anything less I don't want. Anything more you can't give now. So it's an impasse."

"Maybe . . . maybe not." He glanced at the watch on his wrist. "It's getting close to lunch time. What is this advice you want from me?"

Katy pushed back a loose lock of hair, striving to clear her mind of the confusion he had wrought in it. "I know you won't believe it, but I've been given reason to believe you're only likely to be interested in the more obvious kind of woman — and Thalia thinks that as you've so far ignored her, you must have the impression that she's a nice woman at heart, and that's the reason why you haven't made a pass at her."

Charles raised a wry eyebrow. "I shouldn't have made a pass at her even if you hadn't been here," he assured her. "She's not my type."

"I know, but you are her type — the only one present. So if you continue to hold aloof she's going to have a dull time and become increasingly edgy. I should have told her you were my ex-husband from the beginning, but I didn't, and now it's too late. If she'd seen you coming to my cabin, she'd have blown her top and I might have lost my job which, like you, I don't want to give up."

"Correction: I'm not your ex-husband. I'm your husband. What are you asking me to do? Make a pass at Thalia to keep her happy and you employed?"

"No, certainly not. But you could be more careful not to make her suspect there's something between us. And — "

She broke off as a brisk rap was followed by Dr Kent's entrance.

"Charles, d'you think — " he began, stopping short as he caught sight of Katy.

"Oh, I beg your pardon. You're engaged."
Looking embarrassed, he withdrew.

"Oh, dear, what is he going to think?"
Katy murmured anxiously.

"Whatever he thinks, he'll keep his thoughts to himself. Other people's private lives are as safe with David as with a priest," Charles answered calmly. "Anyway, he didn't burst in and catch us *in flagrante delicto.* You're a little more unbuttoned than when you arrived, but compared with the depths of cleavage revealed every day by Miss Martin, yours isn't particularly noticeable."

Katy quickly re-fastened the buttons. "I must go to lunch. I'm sorry I . . . misled you, Charles."

"So am I. I would willingly have missed my lunch for the pleasures I thought were in store for me." His manner was mocking once more. All trace of his deeper feelings was once again hidden behind the sardonic mask.

The next day was Christmas Eve. It seemed strange to spend most of it water-skiing.

The previous Christmas Thalia and Philip had rented a house in the Cotswolds,

153

and Katy had cooked for them and six of their friends. The year before that she had still been working for the agency, and had spent Christmas Day at the home of one of her colleagues. Before that there had been two lonely Christmases on her own in a dreary bed-sitter.

In her father's lifetime, many of her teenage Christmases had been spent in hotels in Austria and Switzerland. Yet, in spite of the lavish presents he had showered on her — and on his current popsie — always there had been something lacking. Never had Christmas been perfect except perhaps long, long ago when her mother had been alive.

As she dressed for dinner that night, thinking about past Christmas Eves, and those to come, she found herself in a strange kind of waking dream in which she was standing outside the railings of a tall, grey-roofed house in Fontainebleau. As if the façade of the house were transparent, or had opened like the door of a doll's house, she found she could see into all the warm, lighted rooms where a large, happy family were busy with the Christmas Eve tasks of dressing the tree and wrapping up last-minute parcels.

In the kitchen, a woman was filling mince pies and listening to a tall, brown-skinned man whose life was spent mostly at sea but who, just now, was home on leave. The man was Charles in ten or fifteen years' time, the first flecks of grey appearing in the hair above his ears, but still lean and fit and virile, and now the Master of *Artemis*. The woman, beloved and contented, was herself at thirty-five or forty.

She roused from this fantasy almost in tears of longing. I could be so happy with that life, she thought wistfully. I should miss Charles horribly when he was away for long periods; but I shouldn't be lonely or bored with all the children around me, and the house and garden to look after. Perhaps, when they were all past babyhood, we could find a kind, reliable French widow who, if he were away for very long, could take my place for a week or two while I came to stay with him in the Captain's quarters.

She told herself sharply to stop it: such a pipe-dream could never come true. And yet why not? Only a few hours earlier, in

155

his cabin, Charles had corrected her when she had referred to herself as his ex-wife; and last night, on the beach, when she had suggested that he might be prepared to release her now, he had not replied that he was, but had asked her if she had a particular reason for wanting to be free.

Having finished making up her face, she rose and went to the wardrobe. But as she reached for the hanger of the dress she had intended to wear, she changed her mind and took out the sea-green chiffon in which she had danced with Charles on their honeymoon at Peñiscola.

The beads on the bodice winked and glimmered in the light as she pressed the bell for the stewardess to come and do her up. Like all *haute couture* dresses at the time she had bought it, the dress fastened not with a zipper but with tiny, chiffon-covered press studs and hooks and eyes made almost invisible by being buttonhole-stitched with matching silk.

"Oh, Miss Brown, what a beautiful colour! It does become you," said her stewardess, when she entered the cabin.

"Thank you. It's quite an old dress, but I've always loved it."

"That's the advantage of a well-made dress such as this. Providing it's looked after properly, it will never wear out and, if the style is simple, it won't go out of fashion either. I've known ladies to wear clothes by Dior and Chanel which they bought ten or fifteen years ago," said the stewardess. "Last year we had a lady on board who had a most lovely dress. Black velvet it was, cut on the bias, with crystal shoulder straps and crystal embroidery down the front. Do you know where she'd bought it? At Sotheby's, the London auction rooms. It was by a designer called Vionnet who was top-notch in the Twenties."

"Really? In that case I needn't feel self-conscious at wearing a four-year-old dress."

"Oh, dear me, no — not at all, miss. There you are."

"Thank you. I'll get my friend Miss Harcourt to unfasten me. It may be the small hours before we come to bed."

"If you should wish to retire before Miss Harcourt, don't hesitate to ring, will you? We shall all be up late tonight, and there's always one stewardess on duty until the last guest has retired."

"Really? That must be rather a weary vigil at times."

"It's not too bad, with the four of us taking it in turns. Years ago, when my mother was a girl, the ladies' maids used to have to sit up every night while the London Season was on. Now that must have been a great trial."

Katy arrived in the saloon to find herself the first there. Instead of putting her hair up, as she had every evening so far, she had left it loose in the style she had worn at nineteen. Catching sight of herself in a mirror, it seemed to her that, physically, she had altered very little since then. The changes were all invisible, but somehow she had to make Charles realise how drastic her transformation had been.

The discovery that she could cook now seemed to have made a slight improvement in his attitude, but not enough — not nearly enough. And there was only one week left. Once Christmas was over, the days would slip by all too fast, with very few opportunities for her to have more than the most casual exchanges with him.

Unless . . . A tremor ran through her. Unless she went to his cabin again, this time to let him make love to her; and then, in the afterglow of their physical reunion, was able to talk to him, and make him understand how much more she had to offer than she had had when he married her.

4

"GOOD evening."

She turned to find Dr Kent near her, the thick pale carpet having muffled his approaching footsteps.

Tonight he was wearing what she took to be the officers' dress uniform. It was white, like their everyday rig, but made of a lightweight material superior to drill, with a high-collared tunic in place of an open-necked shirt.

She returned his smile. "Good evening."

"Where did you learn your expertise on water-skis?" he asked, having seen her flying over the sea, both feet on a single ski, while behind another of the powerboats he had been teaching Thalia how to take off.

"In Spain, a long time ago. We used to spend holidays there."

"'We' being your family?"

"My father. He's dead now."

"I've never been to the western part of the Mediterranean. When I joined *Artemis*, her home berth was Corfu, and the nearest we've ever been to Spain in my time aboard her is Monaco. But Charles knows Spain well, I believe. Maybe he's been to your part of it."

"Possibly. Where did you learn to ski?"

Before he could tell her, they were joined by the Stevensons, followed by a steward proffering the inevitable champagne.

All the passengers had assembled before Charles put in an appearance. The formal uniform with its stiff epaulettes and the gold-embroidered insignia where the collar clipped together under his strong, square chin made him look even more authoritative than he did normally. He looked more like the Captain than the Captain did, thought Katy, waiting for him to catch sight of her looking almost the same as she had on their wedding night.

To her disappointment, she missed his reaction to her appearance because she could not be seen watching him for minutes on end and, whenever it was that he noticed her, she was engaged in conversation.

At dinner, he was on the far side of the table but at the opposite end. When she glanced in his direction, his attention was fully engaged by the people around him.

Dancing with her after dinner, Andreas said, "I watched you skiing this afternoon. You're good at it. So am I. Tomorrow we'll ski together and give these people a show, mm?"

He nodded his head at the others in a manner which carried a suggestion that he and she were two of a kind, and the rest were a different species.

"If you wish," she agreed. "But how do you celebrate Christmas Day? I don't think I'd be at my best soon after a big Christmas lunch."

"No, no, we shall have a light lunch. The Christmas fare will come later. This year, as most of my guests are English and American, the emphasis will be on their traditions. In other years we have had a Franco-Greek Christmas, or some other combination of national customs. Have you any religious beliefs?"

She shook her head. "No, but that doesn't mean I don't respect other people's. If I had children, I think I should make a Nativity scene for them — with those charming little carved wooden figures one can buy in Switzerland — because, whether

162

one believes in God or not, the Bethlehem story is very touching and wonderful. I think one should try to show children as much beauty and goodness as possible before they have to face up to the bad and ugly side of life."

He was dancing with his arm round her, and he drew back to study her face, making her wonder if her remarks had sounded foolishly sentimental.

"Do you like children? Do you want to have a family when you marry?"

Remembering her day-dream earlier, she said, "Yes. Three boys, and three girls."

"You have old-fashioned ideas. Most women don't want more than one or, at the most, two."

"I may never have any," she answered, still half lost in her thoughts.

"You mean you have reason to doubt that you can have children?" asked Andreas.

"Oh, no, I didn't mean that. I — I was only thinking that . . . perhaps . . . "

His laughter rang out, making heads turn. Over his shoulder she caught Carly's green eyes upon her, wondering what she had said to make Andreas bellow with laughter.

"You think you won't find a husband? My dear Katy, there is not an unmarried man on this ship who wouldn't be delighted to father your children for you. How can so lovely a girl be so unassuming? I have never met a beautiful woman as unconscious of her beauty as you are."

"I have reason to know that looks are not enough to hold a man of the kind I want for a husband," she answered, in a subdued tone. "One has to have more than beauty. Intelligence . . . loyalty . . . character."

"And you lack those? I don't believe it."

"Perhaps not now, but when I was several years younger I was very shallow and stupid."

"The young often are. It's forgivable."

"You're very tolerant."

"It's my religion," he said lightly, but she sensed that he meant it seriously.

About half an hour later Charles approached her.

"You said it was a mistake to dance with me," she murmured, as she went into his arms.

He ignored this remark. After some moments, he said, "Haven't I seen the dress you're wearing before?"

"How clever of you to remember. It was part of my trousseau. Three bikinis, this dress, and a nightdress — which I never wore," she added softly.

He slanted a searching glance at her upturned face. "How much champagne have you drunk tonight?"

"Not too much. I never do. One is entitled to be a little . . . frivolous on Christmas Eve, don't you think?"

"Up to a point. But because I sheered off this morning, don't think you can play with fire now, and not get your fingers burnt."

"You asked me to dance with you, Charles."

"It would have looked odd if I hadn't."

"Was that your only reason?"

Again he ignored her remark, and asked, "Why did you put on that dress tonight?"

"Because it's the only one I own which compares with the other women's dresses. Why have I kept it all these years? Because I liked it better than the blue dress I was actually married in, and most women like to keep some memento of their wedding day, even if things go wrong later."

"Your hair is not the way you usually wear it at night. It's as it was on our honeymoon. You look exactly the same as you did then, and I think it's deliberate. Let me warn you again, I'm not the type you can tease with impunity."

I know that, my darling, and before we see another sunrise I'll come to your cabin and let you exact retribution, was her unspoken answer. Some time during dinner she had made up her mind that the only way to break the impasse between them was to start on a physical level and hope to build on that.

Aloud, she said, "But I'm not at all the same, Charles. My exterior may not have changed much but, inside, I'm an almost completely different person from the girl you knew. It's very character-forming, being pitched from a life of luxury to one of comparative penury, and finding out that, even before your father has been convicted, the people you thought were your friends don't want to know you any more. I learnt a lot that first year after Father's arrest. It aged me far more than twelve months. I had been very young for my age, but by the end of that year I'd had to mature in a hurry."

"Yes, it must have been a difficult time for you."

While she was speaking, his previously stern look had softened. But it was not his pity she wanted.

She said, "Charles, last night you asked me if I had a particular reason for wanting my freedom. The answer is No. But would you give it if I wanted it?"

"That would depend on whom you wanted to marry."

"Does being my first husband give you any right to vet my second one?" she asked, her voice very low so that no one could overhear the question.

"Perhaps not, but I should be sorry to see you make a second mistake."

"I don't feel now that I made a mistake the first time. You do, I know, but you could be wrong about that."

Momentarily forgetting the others, she moved her hips closer against him, leaning back on his arm so that she could still look up at him, her lips slightly parted, her eyes soft with mute invitation. She did not feel guilty at tempting him, now that she meant to give herself to him as soon as the party was over.

His fingers tightened on hers, and she saw a muscle working in his cheek, always a sign of repressed impatience or anger.

"You haven't changed all that much, Katy," he told her, his tone clipped. "You still want everything your way. Last time you tried to force me to give up my way of living because it didn't suit you. Now you're doing it again. But, once more, you won't succeed. Chartering wasn't important to me. It was merely a means of earning a living. This job is — very important; and no man worth his salt gives up work he enjoys for the sake of a woman. It may not be in line with current thinking, but I still believe that major adjustments of that kind have to be made by your sex."

"But I agree with you," she answered. "I shouldn't dream of asking you to give up your career for me. I know you couldn't have me on board with you, but we could live together ashore, during your leaves. I could give up my job with Thalia, and find another in France. If not in Fontainebleau, in Paris."

He gave a sardonic laugh. "Do you know

when I had my last leave? Eight months ago. What kind of marriage is that?"

"It's the only kind which you can have until you succeed Commander Longhurst."

"Which I may not. One of the captains of Dracoulis's tankers may be made Captain of *Artemis* when her present one retires, which won't be for quite some time yet. I don't think you're cut out to be a sailor's wife. It's a difficult life for any woman, and doubly so for a young and beautiful one."

"I've managed to live alone for four years. Eight months is nothing compared with four years without love."

"You may not have had a man in your bed during that time, but don't tell me you never had dinner with one."

"No, I have had some dinner dates. Not very many."

"If you were my wife, in fact as well as in name, you wouldn't have any," he replied, on a grim note. "I don't believe in platonic friendships between men and women, and there's no one I'd trust to take you about in my absence."

"I shouldn't need to be taken about. I'd be happy waiting for you. For the first few years I'd be pregnant most of the time. You want children, don't you, Charles?"

Forgetting Thalia, forgetting everything but her love for him, she pressed herself more closely to him, her hand sliding over his shoulder till her fingers touched his bronzed neck.

"For God's sake, Katy! I warned you — "

"And I disregarded your warning. Are you going to punish me for it?" Her smiling eyes met his angry ones without flinching.

The music ended. Charles put her firmly away from him. In an undertone, through clenched teeth, he said, "Yes, and you're not going to like it."

"I may like it very much," she said softly, turning away to find Thalia watching her with a look which would have worried her, had she not had a hopeful feeling that Charles, although furious now, could be won round in the nights which she meant to spend with him.

She passed the rest of the evening longing for bedtime, and wondering how Charles would react when she presented herself at

170

his cabin for her punishment. Somehow she didn't think he would remain angry with her for more than the time it took to wind her arms round his neck and offer him her lips.

But at half past one in the morning when it seemed that at last the party was breaking up, a sudden flash of light followed by a deep booming sound made everyone jump.

"Oh, my God! What was that?" cried Paulette.

It was Charles, already on his feet, who answered her. "An explosion on board the small yacht, Mrs Stevenson."

He and David Kent disappeared, leaving the others to crowd to the railings and gaze in dismay in the direction of the sizeable yacht — but small in comparison with *Artemis* — which during the day had anchored half a mile south.

"Lord! They're on fire, the poor devils," exclaimed Janus, standing next to Katy. "Let's hope they all have the sense to jump overboard."

"Yes," said Andreas, from behind her. "If they do, we can pick them up with little harm done."

"Except that they'll be homeless," said Katy, horrified by the speed with which the flames were engulfing the smaller vessel.

"They'll be alive — that's what matters. Things can be replaced. People can't," he said, in her ear.

Within an incredibly short space of time three boats from *Artemis* were speeding towards the disaster.

In the brilliant Caribbean moonlight it was possible to see that Charles was in charge of the first boat to go to the rescue. The two following boats also had officers in them, but she had not met them. Presumably they were technical officers who did not mingle with the passengers as did the Captain and First Officer.

"Sounds like one of the women having hysterics," said Janus, as a series of high-pitched screams echoed over the sea.

They could see people scurrying about the deck of the burning yacht, and Andreas muttered impatiently, "Why the devil don't they abandon her? There could be another explosion. They can see our men coming to help them. Probably the yacht is on charter, and most of the people aboard her are tourists who panic easily."

"Your First Officer will soon put a stop to that, I imagine," remarked Taylor Stevenson. "We see only his pleasant social face, but I guess in his professional capacity he commands a lot of respect. He looks as if he could be pretty ruthless with troublemakers or hysterical females."

"Yes, he's an excellent officer. Very quick to see what must be done, and completely unflappable," agreed Andreas.

"Your men won't board the yacht, will they? — If there's a chance of another explosion?" Katy asked him anxiously.

"They'll do what they can to save her. They won't take unnecessary risks."

Misunderstanding her look of alarm, he patted her arm and said reassuringly, "You needn't be afraid of a similar outbreak on *Artemis.* We have a highly sophisticated fire prevention system, including alarm bells or automatic sprinklers should the temperature rise above a certain level anywhere on board. One can never say fire is impossible, but if one did occur it would probably be caused by a passenger smoking in bed, and would be confined to that cabin only."

Katy could not reply that it was not her

own safety which concerned her, but that of the men manning the power boats, and particularly of the First Officer. He might not take chances with his men's lives, or risk his own without reason, but the story which Andreas had told her of Charles's rescue of a child from a burning boat in the Pacific confirmed what she had always felt about him: that he would not think of his own skin if a woman or child was in danger. Supposing the screaming woman was trapped below in a cabin?

Having lived in a world without Charles for four long, empty years, the thought that he might now be killed if the yacht blew up with him on board made her start to shiver with terror.

"You are very nervous," said Andreas. "Have you had a bad experience of fire?"

"No, never. I – I just feel so sorry for those people, being shipwrecked on Christmas Eve."

"They're lucky *Artemis* is close by," said Janus. "I've no doubt Dr Kent is all ready to deal with any casualties there may be. Val, you should be in bed, honey."

"I think you should go to bed, too," Andreas told Katy. "There is nothing to be gained by your waking up tired on Christmas Day. Your stewardess can give you something to help you to sleep. There's bound to be a good deal of noise when they bring those people on board. A mild sleeping pill is advisable for everyone tonight."

There was a concerted murmur of agreement from the others.

"Yes, there's nothing we can do to be helpful, so we may as well turn in," said Taylor, addressing his wife.

There was an exchange of goodnights, and the party dispersed.

"Were you a bit tight earlier on?" asked Thalia, when she was in Katy's cabin, unfastening the sea-green dress for her.

Katy turned a puzzled glance on her. Thalia drank gin-and-tonics as freely as she herself drank spa water, but Katy disliked all spirits and was moderate in her consumption of wine. It was not that she lacked the palate to appreciate the fine wines provided by their host, but as several wines were served in the course of each meal, she was careful to avoid having more than one glass of each, and anyone noting her consumption of the champagne which was served between meals would have observed that she drank one glass to everyone else's three or four glasses.

"What makes you ask that?" she asked blankly.

"It wouldn't be surprising as you've never been much of a drinker, and your intake of booze at present must be twice what it normally is."

"What did I do to make you think I was tight?"

"You don't usually drape yourself round your dancing partners quite as freely as you did with Charles Ormond. Carly goes in for that clinging stuff, but I didn't think it was your style."

The fire on the other yacht had driven all thought of the earlier part of the evening out of Katy's head. Now she remembered the rather hostile look Thalia had directed at her after the dance with Charles.

"Goodness, maybe I had had a drop too much," she answered in what she hoped was an airy tone. "Never mind: I expect the First Officer is accustomed to passengers tripping over their own feet, or leaning heavily on him sometimes. Probably he didn't give it a second thought."

"Nevertheless I should watch your step a bit more for the rest of the cruise," said Thalia, with a touch of asperity.

Hating herself for her hypocrisy, Katy looked suitably subdued. "Yes — yes, I will."

"Goodnight."

"Goodnight."

Thalia left the cabin and Katy hung up her dress. But instead of getting ready for bed, she put on a shirt and pants preparatory to going on deck again. She had never taken a sleeping pill in her life, and had no intention of starting now. But she knew she could not go to sleep until she had seen Charles come back on board, safe and unhurt.

After several days on *Artemis* she was beginning to know her way around, and without encountering anyone she made her way to a place on one of the upper decks from where, without being noticed or being in anyone's way, she could keep watch on the gangway at the head of the accommodation ladder.

It was difficult now to make out what was happening on the other vessel which was obscured by clouds of smoke.

Thinking about Thalia's rebuke, Katy wondered if the older girl really had believed she had been three sheets in the wind, as yachtsmen said of a tipsy person. Or had Thalia suspected her of flirting with Charles, and warned her to watch her step with him rather than with alcohol?

A boat appeared round the smokescreen and headed back towards *Artemis*. She was not Charles's boat but one of the others. In place of some of the sailors who had been on board when she set out, and who now must be on the burning yacht, she was full of survivors of the accident.

Stewards and two stewardesses were waiting to look after them as they stepped on *Artemis*'s main deck. All six were middle-aged Americans; three men and three women, presumably husbands and wives. Although shocked, none of them appeared to be hurt.

The next launch to return brought younger people who Katy guessed were the skipper and crew of the other yacht. They had not escaped without injury, and the girl among them — perhaps the cook — was carried up the ladder in the arms of a burly seaman. She appeared to be only half conscious.

It was a long time after that before the third boat returned and, with a deep sigh of relief, Katy saw Charles standing in the stern, his uniform, immaculate earlier, now in a filthy state.

As the launch was lost to her view as it came alongside, she saw Commander Longhurst cross the deck below her to stand by the gangway until Charles reappeared.

"None of the men hurt, Mr Ormond?"

"One or two minor burns. Nothing serious, sir. We've managed to put the fire out, but the damage is very extensive. She'll need a complete refit."

"You'll be glad of a shower, by the look of you."

Charles glanced down at his ruined uniform. "Yes, sir. Rather dirty work, fire-fighting." This reply was accompanied by a flash of white teeth in the sweat-shiny, soot-streaked mask he had acquired.

Satisfied that he had come to no harm, Katy slipped away from her vantage point and returned to her cabin. She had the impression that, while she had been on tenterhooks, Charles had been almost enjoying himself in a situation more to his taste than making small-talk to the Owner's guests. Nevertheless, after cleaning himself, his next need would be sleep, not love. The night was now too far advanced for her to fulfil her intention of going to his cabin. However much Charles might want her, he would not welcome her at this hour, after his strenuous activity on board the other vessel. The surrender by which she hoped to achieve peace between them must be postponed until Christmas night.

She was woken next morning by the sound of an aircraft taking off with, as she learned later, the first batch of people from the wrecked yacht. By lunch time they had all been flown back to Barbados, where their charter had begun.

"It's not that I wish to be inhospitable," Andreas told her. "But I talked to these people last night, and they were a dull lot. I have no desire to spend Christmas Day listening to repeated accounts of what happened to them. Life is too short to suffer bores gladly, but it would have been discourteous to exclude them from our party if they had remained on board. So the solution was to arrange hotel rooms for them, and fly them back to where they came from. They are the sort of people who will greatly enjoy being photographed and interviewed by the local press."

After lunch, he and she and David gave a demonstration of skiing prowess. Andreas skied with the verve of a much younger man. Both Katy and David were good, but he excelled them.

Later in the afternoon, when most of the guests were drowsing under sunbrellas on the beach which, by day, was pale pink, the sand being made of powdered shell rather than the grains of mineral matter of which most European beaches were composed, Katy went swimming by herself. Even without a mask and snorkel, the water was so clear that she could see some of the beautiful fish which lived below the surface.

She had duck-dived to peer at a brilliant blue and yellow Queen Angel-fish which had surprised her by swimming close to inspect her, and had come to the surface to inhale, when a strong hand clamped on her shoulder.

At first she thought it was Andreas, and was surprised to see Charles who had not been with the beach party when she had left them. He must have swum direct from the yacht.

"Oh . . . hello," she said, in surprise, and then the gleam in his eyes sent a tremor of apprehension through her. She had never seen a more obviously punitive light in them.

"Foolish of you, Katy — to think you could get away with baiting me on the dance floor last night," he said softly.

"Aren't you making rather a fuss about nothing?"

They were far too far from the beach for her to have a hope of escaping him, even if his lean brown fingers had not been gripping her shoulder.

"If one lets people get away with things, they try them again," he said dryly.

"Please, Charles — please don't duck me." Although she had no fear of the water itself, she had always hated being ducked.

"Now would I do that when I know how much you dislike it? If you go under, it will be your own fault for struggling." He released her shoulder only to slide his other arm round her waist and draw her against him, her back to his chest. "Just keep still, and nothing alarming will happen to you."

"W-what are you going to do to me?" she stammered nervously.

"What I wanted to do to you last night after your seductive antics on the dance floor."

She gasped. "You can't! People will see."

"They may see our heads together. Providing you don't make a fuss, they won't know what I'm doing to you under the water." As he spoke, he undid the tie at the back of her neck and drew down the top of her bikini, his palms replacing the triangles of cotton.

"Charles! — No!" she implored.

"You used to enjoy my doing this," his mocking voice said in her ear.

"Not like this — in public," she protested. "Oh, you beast . . . you devil . . . how can you?" this as one hand left her breast but only to slide caressingly down to her hip and unfasten the knot securing the bottom of her bikini.

"Don't worry: if it sinks to the bottom I shall do the gentlemanly thing and retrieve it for you," the tormenting voice promised.

She longed to struggle but dared not, afraid that if she did the resultant splashing would attract the attention of the sunbathers on the beach.

"That's right: lie back and enjoy it," he murmured derisively.

Katy gritted her teeth, forcing herself into passivity while he kept them afloat by treading water, and his hands wandered over her body, tracing slow circles on her breasts and stomach until she was no longer quivering with rage but with the beginnings of the excitement he knew so well how to induce.

As his caresses became increasingly sensuous, one last futile surge of resistance made her snatch at his hand with both of hers, and strike at his shins with her heels. But even with both hands she could not restrain the strength of his sinewy wrist, and her kicks missed their targets.

"I shall never forgive you for this, Charles," she told him hoarsely, and the next instant groaned as a new wave of pleasure engulfed her.

All at once she was free. The hard wall of chest and shoulder which had been behind her had gone. The arms which had been on either side of her were there no more. The fingers, gentle while she submitted, relentless if she resisted, were no longer at work on the sensitive parts of her body, making her shudder with ecstasy.

"Now perhaps you know how a man feels when a woman tantalises him."

She opened her eyes to find Charles a couple of yards away, his grey gaze meeting her dazed one with a glitter of unkind amusement.

She saw him inhale and disappear. A few seconds later he passed her under the water. When he came up on the other side of her he said, "You're a trifle dishevelled, but you haven't lost anything."

He began to swim back to the yacht, leaving Katy smouldering with mingled rage and self-loathing. She had never felt more humiliated. This had not been like the night in her cabin when his caresses had been accompanied by kisses, when he had shared in the tempest of feeling which Thalia's tap had interrupted before it could engulf them both. This had been altogether different because it was only she who had been carried away. He had remained a spectator, stripping her of all dignity by watching her transports instead of sharing them.

It took less than a minute to rearrange her bikini, but much longer to recover from the high pitch of excitement to which he had brought her, and in which feverish state he had left her.

As she swam about, waiting to calm down before rejoining the beach party, all the anxiety she had felt for him the night before, all her loving intentions towards him, were swamped by the strength of her present sense of outrage.

When at length she emerged from the water, at first it seemed that no one on the beach had seen Charles swim towards her, stay with her, and then swim away.

But as she sank into a deck chair to let her skin dry by evaporation, Carly said, in a sugary voice, "Was that Charles who swam out to talk to you in the sea about fifteen minutes ago? At this distance, I couldn't be sure."

"Yes, it was," Katy answered casually.

"What an odd place to have a chat. Very private, of course." Carly's eyes were concealed by her sun-glasses, but Thalia's were not and Katy saw the designer's vividly blue gaze turn searchingly in her direction.

She felt herself starting to flush, and was relieved when David Kent rose from his chair nearby, and said, "I'm going for a stroll round the island. Would you care to join me, Katy?"

"Yes, I should like to," she said instantly, glad to escape Carly's obvious desire to make trouble.

As she and the doctor walked away, she heard the actress say to Thalia, "Quite a femme fatale, your little friend. All the officers seem to fancy her."

David also heard the remark. He said, "Does that sort of bitchiness bother you? I shouldn't let it, if I were you. Miss Martin is probably piqued because she's not having too much success in her quarter."

Katy said, "I don't mind Carly being catty." On impulse, she added, "As long as it doesn't upset Thalia."

"Which it might, as Thalia fancies Charles and wouldn't take kindly to him being more interested in you?"

She had not realised he was so shrewd an observer of undercurrents. "I should think it's not uncommon for passengers to fancy the First Officer, but I doubt if he often returns their interest," she said off-handedly.

"No, you're right. In general, he doesn't," David agreed. "He's married. Did you know that?"

"Yes, but separated, I believe."

"He was separated. I have an idea that he and his wife may have met again, and that's why he's noticeably uptight at present."

Could it be that, after finding her in Charles's cabin, the doctor had guessed the truth of their relationship? Or was she reading too much into a remark which might not mean that at all?

She said only, "Is he?" and waited for his next remark.

"Yes, I noticed it as soon as I came back on board. Charles is normally very relaxed. During my absence, something happened to put him on edge." He paused. "Perhaps he'd had a letter from her."

"Are you in his confidence? Has he discussed his marriage with you?"

188

"No, never. He's not the confiding type. I should think she must have been a very special kind of girl to capture his fancy."

"Perhaps she only seemed special at first. She didn't keep him, did she?"

"Maybe that was his fault. He's a very good First Officer but perhaps not so good as a husband."

"No, it was her fault, not his. The blame was all hers," said Katy.

He stopped walking and turned to face her. "Do you know her? Is that what's upset him, meeting a friend of his wife's?"

"Not a friend of his wife's. His wife. But I think you'd guessed that, hadn't you?"

"It seemed a strong possibility," he admitted. "In the ordinary way if a passenger went to his cabin she wouldn't remain there for long. And the atmosphere was fairly electric when I intruded on you yesterday. It must have been quite a shock to meet again unexpectedly."

"It was — a tremendous shock. We'd been out of touch for four years. He might have been dead, for all I knew."

"Tell me to mind my own business if you want to, but I like Charles and I admire him, so I can't help being curious. Is there anything left of what you once had between you?"

"I don't know," she answered slowly. "Sometimes I think I still love him, and sometimes he makes me hate him" — remembering the deliberately lascivious movements of his hands, and the cold mockery in his eyes when, having aroused her, he had left her. "Have you ever loved anyone, David?"

"Not very seriously, so far. I would rather not meet my fate for a year or two," he answered lightly. "For the time being I like being at sea, but it wouldn't fit in with being married."

"No, that seems to be what Charles feels, and I wouldn't ask him to give up his career on my account. I'm afraid there's no future for us. It's a pity we had to meet again — it's only re-opened old wounds," she said, with a sigh. "I suppose it's because you're a doctor that I feel I can talk to you about it. Normally I'm not given to confiding my troubles, any more than Charles is."

"In that case I'll indulge my curiosity and ask what went wrong between you."

She gave him a brief account of her shortcomings as Charles's bride.

"You take all the blame on yourself, but in my observation when a marriage breaks down there are usually faults on both sides," was David's comment.

"No, not in this case. It was my fault. I was spoiled beyond any man's bearing."

"You must have changed a great deal. According to your stewardess, you're one of the most courteous, considerate passengers she's ever looked after. She was singing your praises at some length while she was collecting some pills for one of her colleagues this morning. 'A very neat and tidy and sympathetic young lady, with manners as nice as her smile' were her exact words."

"Goodness!" said Katy, taken aback and rather embarrassed at having this encomium reported to her.

"I've heard similar things from other people. You do have a winning smile, Katy, as I noticed when I first met you; not the kind of smile which goes with a hard, selfish nature."

"I hope I'm not selfish now, but I was at the time when Charles knew me."

191

"I don't suppose he was perfect. None of us are."

"No, but he was perfect for me, if I'd had sense to adapt myself. Now that I'm ready to do that, it's no longer possible, or rather he feels that it isn't."

"He may yet change his mind about that. Seeing you every day — swimming with you, dancing with you — could weaken even Charles's iron will," David said encouragingly.

For the rest of their walk they spoke of other, less personal matters, and it was not until later Katy realised that talking to David had calmed her, and soothed the rawness of the mortification she had felt after Charles's behaviour in the sea.

She wondered if David would tell Charles he knew about their marriage, and if he might also put in a good word for her. Not that Charles was likely to be influenced by anyone else's judgment of her.

As she lay in her bath, before dressing for Christmas night, it still seemed to Katy that her only chance of reviving the love he had felt once was to let him make love to her, and hope that the physical relationship would bring to life love in the fuller sense.

Thus it was that when she and her husband saw each other again in the saloon before dinner, she returned his sardonic smile with a friendly one and, although her colour rose and her skin tingled where his licentious hands had provoked her unwilling response, there was no lingering flicker of anger in her hazel eyes as they met his.

"Merry Christmas, Charles," she said warmly, and had the gratification of hearing a hint of surprise in his answering greeting.

Knowing in advance the number but not the sex of the other people who had been invited on the cruise, Thalia and Katy had prepared presents suitable for either men or women. However, although Katy had had the forethought to wrap two or three extra presents to give to her cabin attendant and anyone else with whom she might be in close contact, she had not anticipated that the Captain and two of his officers would be of the party. However, as she had no relations and only a small circle of friends for whom to indulge in the pleasures of Christmas shopping, after buying her main present for Thalia, she had added a number of other, lesser gifts.

In the circumstances she felt justified in giving three of these afterthoughts to the three officers. Luckily they were not the sort of things which could only be given to a woman.

One was a small rosewood box, equally suitable for holding ear-rings or cuff-links, and this she had relabelled for the Captain. Another was an Indian paperweight which would do for the doctor; and for Charles there was a silk square, black and white with a Paisley design which made it an acceptable scarf for a man to knot round his neck with any casual shirt.

Whereas Katy's presents were modest, except for the malachite obelisk she had bought for Thalia who collected the stone, those given by all the other guests were far more lavish, and the presents bestowed by their host were lavish in the extreme.

Katy gasped when she found herself the recipient of a gold bracelet. As her present to Andreas was a book of photographs of sea-birds in flight — it had been difficult to choose a present for one of the world's richest men — she found his generosity embarrassing. But nobody else seemed disturbed by the costliness of his gifts.

Thalia had received a platinum chain with her initial, studded with sapphires, as a pendant. Carly was exulting over a luxurious dressing-case and matching make-up case. To his daughter, Andreas had given an antique emerald necklace with ear-rings to match.

Soon the saloon, with its two silver-decorated live Christmas trees, was bestrewn with expensive wrappings which would, no doubt, be cleared away by the stewards while the guests were having dinner.

It was at the end of dinner that, at the head of the table, Andreas suddenly rose to his feet and announced, "Ladies and gentlemen, I am very delighted to tell you that my daughter and Alain are engaged to be married. Let us drink to their happiness."

While everyone but the young couple pushed back their chairs and raised their glasses, Alain took Arianna's hand and slipped on her finger a solitaire diamond ring of impressive size and fire.

But it was the way he kissed her hand and the look her gave her as he did it which made Katy experience a tightness in her throat as she joined in the toast.

The Greek girl's shining dark eyes and her brilliant smile were a poignant reminder of Katy's own feeling of radiance when she and Charles had announced their love to the world.

He did not dance with her that night but, at one point, he sat down beside her, and said, "Thank you for the scarf. I'm sorry I have nothing to give you."

There was no one else near at that moment. Katy said, "You could give me back *In The South Seas*" — referring to a pocket edition of a book by Robert Louis Stevenson which she had seen in his cabin, and which had once belonged to her. "But not if you sometimes re-read it, or if you have other reasons for keeping it."

"I'll have it delivered to your cabin. Or would you prefer me to bring it in person?"

Suddenly, unseen by the other, his compelling pewter-coloured eyes were alight with the same sensual gleam which had been in them that afternoon.

He appraised her bare golden shoulders and the low décolletage of her inexpensive short evening dress of thin Indian cotton, printed in aubergine on lilac.

She felt herself starting to blush. "Please, Charles — " she began.

"You mean 'Yes, please, Charles'?" he asked mockingly.

"No! That is, yes, but not to come to my — "

"You seem a trifle uncertain. This afternoon you said you would never forgive me."

"This afternoon you behaved like a brute . . . a pirate," she added, remembering Andreas's term for him.

He said carelessly, "Women like a little brute force. It gratifies their streak of masochism."

"Or at least that's what men like to believe, in order to justify their sadistic streak."

"Become a feminist, have you, Katy?"

"Not at all. I just don't like having things done to me against my will. You've never experienced being helpless. You'd dislike it even more than I do."

From cheekbone to chin his darkly-tanned skin seemed to tighten. He said, in a low, bitter tone, "You don't know what you're talking about. My will counts for nothing every time I come near you.

You have only to look at me to make me react as I made you react this afternoon. Try to imagine that, my girl."

"I can, and there's a remedy."

"Yes, but not one you find acceptable."

"Perhaps — " She broke off, seeing Spyros approaching.

He asked her to dance, and she had no choice but to accept. It was maddening to have been interrupted just at that moment, but if anything had been needed to reaffirm her decision to give Charles what he wanted, and what she hoped would lead to a happy outcome for them both, it was the low, impassioned tone in which he had said, 'My will counts for nothing every time I come near you'.

It was before midnight when she noticed that Alain and Arianna were no longer present, but had slipped away to conclude the evening à deux. About half past twelve the Captain retired, followed shortly afterwards by Charles.

Katy was dancing with David when she heard her husband saying goodnight to people. She wondered how long she should wait before following him, and decided that half an hour should be enough. Even on

Christmas night, there might be checks he had to make before turning in. He might have a nightcap with the Captain. He would be sure to have a shower.

To wash himself night and morning had been his invariable habit in all the time they had lived together. The clean male scent of his skin was something she had never forgotten. He might have changed in other ways but not, she felt sure, in the fastidious cleanliness which had made him always pleasant to be near in a climate where, sometimes, some men were not.

Having said her goodnights, not to everyone, but to those who were near her, she went directly to Charles's cabin. She had taken her presents to her own cabin shortly after dinner, at the same time repainting her lips and refreshing her scent.

She knew there was little danger of encountering anyone on her way. Apart from one steward on duty, and such members, if any, of the crew who had necessary functions to perform, the rest of the yacht's complement would be enjoying their festivities somewhere below.

That the Captain might be having a

nightcap in Charles's quarters was a risk she had to take. It seemed unlikely, if Commander Longhurst's accommodation was by far the more comfortable and spacious.

Without knocking, she opened the door and stepped quickly inside. The cabin was in darkness, and no sounds came from the adjoining bathroom. Katy felt for the switch plate, and turned on the bedside reading light and another above the built-in desk.

Half an hour later, still waiting, she turned back the cover on Charles's bunk and kicked off her shoes. For a while she attempted to re-read *In The South Seas*. The book had a leather binding and, inside, the pleasant smell of old paper. Always attracted by tales of faraway places, she had bought it in a second-hand bookshop in the country town near her boarding school.

She remembered reading, for the first time, on the first page, the lines which she read again now. *For nearly ten years,* Stevenson had written, *my health had been declining . . . I chartered accordingly Dr Merrit's schooner yacht, the* Casco, *seventy-four tons register; sailed from*

San Francisco towards the end of June 1888 . . . and reached Samoa towards the close of '89. By that time gratitude and habit were beginning to attach me to the islands . . .

Katy's gaze wandered off the page as she thought of Charles in the South Seas and how, given more common sense, she might have shared that experience.

Oh, Charles — hurry, darling! she thought.

Tonight, no book in the world could hold her attention. She was consumed with impatience for the door to open, and her husband to find her waiting for him.

She was woken from a deep sleep by being lifted up in strong arms. Still no more than half awake, she realised the arms were her husband's, and said drowsily, "I thought you were never coming."

"Do you realise what time it is? What are you doing here?" he asked, holding her to his chest as easily as if she were a sleepy child.

"I've been waiting for you. Where've you been?" she asked, swallowing a yawn.

"Yarning with the Captain. He gets

lonely at this time of year — misses his wife and likes to talk. But if I'd known you were here — "

"Darling Charles, do you miss me sometimes?" she murmured, slipping her arms round his neck.

For an instant she thought he was going to kiss her, and her lips parted slightly in readiness. But as his head bent towards hers, he jerked it back. "This is no time to go into that. It's four o'clock in the morning, and I'm not a passenger. I can't sleep late tomorrow, I have to be up early. Besides which, I'm not quite sober, and you're half asleep. Tomorrow is another night. For the moment it's back to your cabin with you."

"But, Charles, I want to stay here!"

"You can't. Not tonight, my lovely. Be quiet now. We don't want to wake people."

Before she could utter another protest he had left the cabin and was carrying her along the corridor. She leaned her head against his shoulder, thinking that if, as he claimed, he had had one or two drinks too many, it had not affected his balance. His grip was firm, his gait steady.

It was she who felt fuddled, not from wine but from sleep.

Outside her cabin he set her down, and the kiss he had withheld before came down hard on her unresisting lips.

"Until tomorrow," he murmured, and she watched him striding away until his tall figure had swung out of sight round the corner.

When she opened the door of her cabin, her mind was too full of his kiss to be immediately aware of the alien smell of cigarette smoke, or to feel surprise that her light was on. When she saw the two dozing women, one stretched on the bed, the other lolling in the armchair, she thought for an instant Charles had left her at the wrong door, and this was Thalia's cabin, not her own.

Then she saw that it was her own cabin, and took in the stub-piled ashtrays and the unfinished drinks. Suddenly very wide awake, she closed the cabin door behind her, and nudged the actress's outstretched foot with her own. "Wake up, Miss Martin."

Carly murmured something, then roused and opened her eyes. At four o'clock in the morning, her make-up had long lost its freshness and the skin round her eyes was puffy. Her face looked a decade older than her body.

"So you're back," she remarked unpleasantly.

Her voice woke Thalia, who sat up.

"What are you both doing in here?" asked Katy, crossing to the ports to let out the fug of stale smoke.

"What have *you* been doing is the question. Whose cabin have you been in?" Thalia asked sharply.

When Katy didn't reply, she went on, "We thought you weren't coming back, but since you have, you'd better come clean. Have you been with Charles, or Andreas — or perhaps with your latest conquest, David Kent?"

As the two older women regarded her with hostile eyes, Katy felt as if she were in a cage with two enraged tigresses.

"With Charles," she answered. "But — "

"You damned little bitch!" Thalia spat at her.

Carly looked relieved. She said, "I'm going to bed. Goodnight, Thalia."

"Goodnight," the designer said curtly.

Her blue eyes were fixed on Katy with the basilisk glare of a woman wild with jealous temper. Scarcely had Carly left them before she burst out, "My God! Did I make a mistake in treating you as my friend, instead of as the hired help! Philip told me once that he thought there was something devious about you — that you weren't quite as sweet and saintly as you made out. How right he was! After seeing your performance on this trip, I'm only surprised you never had a crack at him. From the minute we set foot on board, you've been after Charles Ormond like a mongoose after a snake. I didn't notice it at first, but other people did — *and* the way you've played up to Andreas!"

This was only the beginning of a tirade such as Katy had never heard before. She had known about Thalia's temper, and that she could, on occasion, use some hair-raising adjectives. Katy's father had not been a man who censored his language when women were present. But the gross invective which Thalia flung at her now went beyond the four-letter words in use in her set. Not only the way she expressed herself, but the coarseness of the thoughts expressed, shocked Katy into stupefied silence. She had had no notion that someone as exceptionally gifted and successful as Thalia could, beneath a confident exterior, be so profoundly insecure that even the fact that her cook had been to a finishing school filled her with festering resentment.

The effect of this violent outburst was not to make her defend herself, but rather to shrink with distaste from responding at all.

"If you think, you slut, that we can go on as before, you're very much mistaken," stormed Thalia. "Your frolics are over, so get packed. Tomorrow morning you'll be leaving, and I don't want to see you again!"

After she had gone, Katy sat down on the dressing-stool and, perfectly calmly, began to take off her make-up which, being much lighter than Carly's, did not, she was relieved to see, make her look as jaded. Perhaps it was because it was not the first time that her future had blown up in her face that she could accept Thalia's dismissal without much dismay. It had been a good job but, even without a reference, she felt confident of finding another, equally good.

It was not difficult to visualise the circumstances which had led up to Thalia's tirade. She must have come to the cabin, perhaps to discuss the opulence of Andreas's presents, found Katy not there and instantly become suspicious. Had she known where Charles was quartered, her jealousy — fanned by Carly — might have driven her to confirm her suspicions immediately. Not knowing where to find him, she must have decided to wait for Katy's return and then, bored with waiting on her own, called Carly to keep her company. After which, several strong gin-and-tonics on top of the drinks consumed earlier had caused them both to nod off, hence the scene on Katy's return.

That Thalia would enforce her threat to make Katy leave the next day seemed doubtful. It was difficult to see how she could make her go, and Katy had no intention of being harassed into leaving voluntarily. For one thing she was not guilty of the designer's charge that she had deliberately filched Charles, and made bedroom eyes at every man on the ship.

This was the exaggerated ranting of someone quite unbalanced by jealousy.

If I didn't love Charles, I should leave — willingly, thought Katy, as she brushed her teeth. But I'm not going to lose the chance of spending another five days with him, even if Thalia and Carly do look daggers at me from now on.

After Thalia's display of fishwifery, she had no confidence that the designer would try to conceal her animosity in the way that a well-bred person would in the same situation.

Not that I can claim to be that, Katy reminded herself. At least Thalia's father was an honest man, which is more than can be said of mine.

She wondered if, to spare the rest of the cruise party the embarrassment of witnessing Thalia's ire, Charles might be willing to tell her, in confidence, the truth. Somehow Katy did not think he would. He was the kind of man who, if falsely accused of some disreputable act, would react with disdainful silence; and would expect the same reaction from others.

She remembered his swift, hard kiss,

and the promise implicit in his murmured 'Until tomorrow'.

By this time tomorrow night, Thalia's charge that she had been to bed with him would be justified. On this happy, hopeful thought, Katy fell asleep.

She was woken up by her stewardess who, when she opened her eyes, said, "I'm sorry to disturb you, Miss Brown, but it's on Mr Dracoulis's instructions, as you might say. He would like you to join him for drinks in his private quarters at midday, and it's nearly half past eleven now. I thought you would want at least half an hour to get ready."

"Yes . . . yes, thank you."

"Shall I run a bath, or would you prefer to have a shower?"

"Oh . . . a shower, I think. A cold shower will wake me up. I was . . . reading until very late, or rather until very early. That's why I've overslept."

"You haven't overslept, miss. There are several ladies and gentlemen still in bed. You won't want much breakfast, I expect, but when you've come out of the shower would you like just a glass of orange juice

209

and perhaps a fresh roll and butter — to give you something inside you before you have drinks before lunch."

Katy accepted this suggestion, and was soon standing under a refreshing jet of cool water. When, wrapped sarong-wise in a bath sheet, with her wet hair turbanned in a smaller towel, she returned to the bedroom, the chilled orange juice was waiting for her. It was on a tray with an organdie cloth and a small vase containing one rose. Pretty, hand-embroidered cloths, crystal specimen vases, heavy solid silver cutlery and elegant china accompanied everything served in the cabins on *Artemis.* She was ready at two minutes to twelve, and made her way to the Owner's suite, expecting to find others there, and wondering how Thalia would act.

But when a steward opened the door and ushered her through the lobby to the spacious study, she was either the first to arrive or no one else had been invited. The grey-haired Greek was sitting alone on the balcony.

He rose. "Good morning, Katy. What would you like to drink?"

She asked for Campari and soda and,

when they were alone, said, "I'd like to thank you again for this beautiful bracelet."

"And I you for this," he replied.

With surprise she noticed that the book he had laid aside when she joined him was the book of sea-birds. He took it up and turned the pages to show her a photograph he thought particularly fine. Then he laid it aside for the second time and said, "I have asked the others to join us at one o'clock, but first I have something to tell you . . . and something to ask."

5

"SOMETHING to tell me?" she queried.

"Miss Harcourt — and Miss Martin also — are no longer with us," said Andreas. "Perhaps you didn't hear the plane leaving. It took off about an hour ago. They should by now be in Barbados."

Katy stared at him in bewilderment. "Why did they leave?"

"Because I felt they were not enjoying the cruise as much as they had hoped, and when people are not enjoying themselves they can mar the pleasure of others," he answered.

"Perhaps you should have sent me away. It was I who was marring their pleasure."

"But not mine, Katy. I like you — better than I liked either of them."

She was not certain what to say to this, and finally settled for, "Thalia was your daughter's guest, and I'm just . . . an appendage. Won't Arianna be put out?"

"For the time being my daughter has eyes for no one but Alain. She would not care if everyone left," was his reply. "Carly Martin came at my invitation but, to be frank, I find myself suddenly very weary of her kind of woman. And she wasn't a woman's woman. The other three didn't like her — Valentina, Paulette and my sister-in-law. Those who remain will get on more comfortably without the two who have left."

"You know, I imagine, that Thalia was very . . . annoyed. In fact she has sacked me."

"So I understand. Is being unemployed, even temporarily, going to spoil the rest of your holiday?"

"No, I shan't have too much trouble in finding another post. But I'm sorry my association with her has ended like this, with bad feeling."

"That brings me to what I wish to ask you. I'd like to hear your side of the story."

"May I ask what Thalia's side was?"

"Certainly: she came to me early this morning to say that, for reasons she preferred not to disclose, it was advisable for you to return to England — at once. When I pressed her, she said you had been drinking more than was good for you, and embarrassing her by pursuing two of my officers." He smiled. "I presume she meant Mr Ormond and young Dr Kent. I found the notion of their needing to be protected from your advances rather humorous, particularly where Ormond is concerned. The truth of the matter, I fancy, is that he has been paying more attention to you than to her."

"To some extent — yes," she agreed. "But as you've already formed your opinion, I feel all I need to say is 'thank you' for not thinking the worst of me."

Andreas said, "I prefer the evidence of my own eyes to anyone else's possibly distorted view of a situation. You eat and drink with enjoyment, but never to excess, I have noticed. As for Ormond and Kent, it's plain for anyone to see that they both find you attractive. But although you seem to like Kent, once or twice I have seen you looking dubiously at Mr Ormond. Perhaps I overstated my warning about him."

"I like Dr Kent very much," Katy

agreed readily. "Mr Ormond can be rather ... intimidating at times."

"But never importunate, I hope?" he said, watching her closely.

She remembered the things Charles had done to her only the previous afternoon. Where had Andreas been at that time? Not on the beach with the others, so he must have been somewhere on board. The spot where her husband had ambushed her was not within view of the balcony deck where they were sitting at this moment, and perhaps not in view of any part of the ship where, with the aid of field glasses, someone would have been able to see the First Officer untying the knot of a female passenger's halter.

"Oh, no — no, never," she answered, with more haste than truth. "I — I think the fact of the matter was not that Mr Ormond has paid much attention to me, but that he paid none to Thalia. She's not very happy at the moment, and finding him very attractive she was hoping for a shipboard romance to cheer herself up."

"I'm sure you're right. I came to a similar conclusion — but I phrased it less euphemistically," he added dryly. "I should doubt that Miss Harcourt's attitude to men is any more romantic than mine towards women."

"But you loved your wife . . . your first wife."

"Ah, yes, but I was young then. Now I am like Rudolf Bing who, when he was General Manager of the Metropolitan Opera in New York, and had been having an argument with the late Maria Callas, said of himself, 'People don't understand my true nature. Beneath this rugged exterior beats a heart of pure stone'."

"I'm sure your heart isn't stony," she protested.

"It is, my dear. I can be kind — when it suits me. But as I have just demonstrated with your former employer, if anyone bores or annoys me, I become implacable. Tell me, what precipitated Miss Harcourt's desire to rid herself of competition?"

Katy wondered if it could possibly have come to his ears that, twice, she had been to Charles's cabin. She was almost sure her visits had been unobserved, except by Dr Kent, but how could she be certain? If Andreas knew she was not being entirely frank with him, would he send her packing like Thalia? Yet Charles, who had not invited either of her visits, although he had not seemed displeased by the second one, might not wish the Owner to know she had been to his quarters; and her first loyalty must be to Charles.

Not wishing to be devious, she took the only other course, and said, "Please . . . I would so much rather not talk about it. I can honestly say that what Thalia suspected was *not* true. I had not been wilfully poaching on her preserves. I should never do that."

For a nervous moment she thought he might be going to insist that she went into details. But at length he nodded, accepting her reserve. "I believe you. We will put this little unpleasantness out of our minds."

"How will you explain it to the others?"

"I shall say that both my departed guests have received an urgent summons in connection with their professional lives. No one will believe me, but they won't say so. With regard to your professional life, would you care to work for me?"

"For you?" she echoed blankly.

"I believe you have met Madame Jourdain who runs my domestic affairs with such

217

efficiency. Her retirement is not too far distant. Shortly, she will have to begin the search for a suitable successor. Do you think you could tackle the job?"

"I — I don't know," Katy stammered.

"Then why not try it for a period? This cruise ends on the second of January when I and the rest of the party will fly back to Europe or America, and *Artemis* will return to the Mediterranean. I shall rejoin her when she reaches the south of Spain where one of my companies is building a new harbour and holiday complex. By that time we should know if you are equal to replacing Madame Jourdain when she retires."

Katy was still nonplussed by a turn of events which could transform Thalia's dismissal of her from a distressing surprise into the best thing which had ever happened to her. When Madame Jourdain had mentioned her approaching retirement, it had not even crossed Katy's mind that she might apply for the post. Apart from being contracted to work for Thalia for at least another eight months, she would not have felt herself to be sufficiently experienced to apply for what must surely be one of the pinnacles of her profession, and one not usually attained by anyone under the age of thirty, or even forty.

"I don't know what to say," she confessed.

Andreas said, "The others will be joining us in a moment or two. Think it over for a few days. There is no hurry. Let me know your decision on New Year's Eve."

Neither the Captain nor Charles joined the rest of the party for drinks, or for the light luncheon which followed. In the absence of two of the women guests, their presence was no longer necessary from the point of view of *placement*. Did this mean they would not appear again? Katy wondered, rather anxiously. To be free of Thalia's watchful glances was no advantage if Charles was not going to be present.

She spent the afternoon lying by the pool, alternately dozing in the sun and cooling off in the water. In her hearing, the three other women made no reference to the two who had gone, but she guessed that they had, or would do so when she was not there.

The fact that, as she had surmised, neither the Captain nor the First Officer was present at dinner would have spoilt

Katy's evening had she not, an hour before dinner, received a note. It had been unsigned, and consisted of a single line.

I'll be with you at 2300.

At half past ten, when Valentina announced that she was going to bed early, Katy said, "I think I will, too."

In her cabin she had a shower, with a cap on to keep her hair dry. She had with her a pretty wrapper of tiny-patterned blue and white cotton, ruffled at the neck and the elbows, with a full skirt flaring from a slightly high waist. Having sprayed herself from head to foot with *Dioressence*, one of her Christmas presents, she put on the wrapper and fastened the sash. Charles had only to tug one of the tails and she would be naked and scented and eager in his arms. The thought made her draw in a quivering breath of excitement.

He came on the dot of eleven, stepping swiftly inside and closing the door as he had the first time he came to her.

Katy had been looking out of a port until the sound of the door opening had made her swing round to face him. As before he took off his hat and tossed it aside.

"Come here," he commanded softly.

220

Three swift steps, and she was in his arms. Her parted lips trembled for an instant before they were crushed beneath his in a kiss to which, now, she could respond without restraint, her body pliant against his, her eyes closed in total surrender.

After a while he swung her up into his arms, as he had the night before. He carried her to the bed and laid her upon it. When she opened her eyes, he was unbuttoning his shirt, his fingers clumsy with haste, his grey eyes hot and devouring as he looked at her supine figure and, because their feverish embrace had loosened her wrapper, took in the half exposed breast and the smooth line of golden thigh exposed to his hungry gaze.

As he dealt with his cuffs, she said, "Darling, such wonderful news! Andreas has offered me the chance to take over from Madame Jourdain. What could be more perfect for us? We can be together all the time."

"What?" His movements suddenly arrested, he looked at her with the beginning of a frown between his dark brows.

"You knew that Andreas had sent Thalia

away — and Carly as well — didn't you?"

His frown deepened. "I knew he'd got rid of the actress. I thought Thalia had left for some purpose of her own, and would be rejoining us. All these people flit about the world the way ordinary mortals catch buses. The fact that you were still here suggested that she'd be back on board in a day or two."

"Oh, no — she's gone back for good. Having sacked me because of you."

"Because of me?" he said blankly.

"After you left me last night, I found Thalia and Carly in here, waiting for me. Thalia demanded to know where I'd been, and I had to admit I'd been with you. She lost her temper and said things which would have made it impossible for us ever to be friendly again, even if she hadn't sacked me. I was rather shattered at the time, but now — "

She sprang from the bed and flung her arms round him, pressing her cheek against him where the unbuttoned shirt bared the hard brown wall of his chest.

"Of course it all depends on my being capable of doing Madame Jourdain's job, but I'm sure I can. I'm certain of it."

She lifted her face, smiling at him, one hand slipping inside his shirt to stroke his smooth skin which felt quite different from her own because his covered bone and muscle and nowhere was soft and yielding like feminine flesh. He was all male, her tall, strong husband. Even his heartbeats felt different, pounding against her palm like the powerful thumps of a pile-driver.

"Kiss me again," she whispered, with half closed eyes.

Instead he captured her hand and put her a little away from him. "You haven't explained why Dracoulis got rid of Thalia. Did you go to him and ask him to?"

"No, no — as if I would, Charles! She went to him, hoping to get rid of me. But he didn't believe her accusations that I'd been drinking too much, and making up to all the men. If she hadn't still been wild with temper, she would have seen that he wouldn't. But I think Thalia's one of those people who become unbalanced by jealousy. Anyway, she's gone now. Don't let's waste time talking about her. We're together again, at long last." She gave him an impish look through lowered lashes.

"Don't you want to finish what you began in the sea? You'll find me much more cooperative."

But no grin changed the stern line of his mouth at this reminder of what he had done to her in the water, nor did he sweep her back into his arms. With puzzled dismay, she saw that the passion which had blazed between them in his first few minutes in the cabin had now, on his side, died down, or been quenched in some way.

"What is it?" she asked. "Why do you scowl?"

"I don't want you working on *Artemis*. It would be an impossible situation. You must tell Dracoulis you don't want the job."

"But I do want it — very much. I haven't yet told him about us, but I'm sure when he knows we're married he won't object. Why should he?"

"He may not, but I do. I have no intention of allowing my life to be disrupted a second time."

"Disrupted? Why should I disrupt it? I want to *complete* your life, Charles."

"I thought I'd made it clear that the only

224

relationship I consider possible between us is a strictly temporary one."

"You said so at first — yes. But since then — "

"That's still my opinion," he told her. "I want you, but not on a permanent basis. We've tried that. It didn't work then, and it wouldn't work now."

"Aren't you even willing to try it?"

"No, I'm sorry, Katy, I'm not. You must face the fact that all we have in common is that" — with a gesture at the bed behind her. "That's really all we ever did have and, if you hadn't been a virgin when we met, which made me feel I had to marry you, we could have had a good time together without all the trouble which followed."

"Oh, no, Charles — no! That's not true," she protested. "We had more in common than you'll admit. If only I'd been then as I am now, the chartering business could have been very successful. Our passengers would have been the best-fed charter parties in the Mediterranean."

"Perhaps, but I'm not in the charter game any more, and here your talents in that line have no scope as far as I'm personally concerned. Your presence on board could only diminish my efficiency."

"Why? I should be busy myself much of the time. We'd see very little of each other except when we were both off duty."

"On any ship the second in command, even more than the captain, is virtually always on duty; and, on a ship like this one, there are social duties as well. There's no place and no time for a wife in my life now."

"Commander Longhurst used to have his wife on board."

"Yes, but she was a placid, retiring woman who was happy writing letters to her daughters, and knitting things for her grandchildren. She was about as undemanding as it's possible to be. We scarcely knew she was on board."

Katy saw that argument was futile. She could talk for an hour and not budge him an inch from his conviction. But there were other means of persuasion which, because she was sure he was wrong, and they could be happy together, she would not scruple to use.

"In that case we'd better make the most of such things as we do have in common," she said, smiling again, although most of the joy she had felt on receiving his note had drained out of her since his cold reception of her — as she had thought — wonderful news.

Her hands went to the waist of her robe and a moment later she made one swift, supple movement and the wrapper fell round her feet, leaving her naked.

The action instantly rekindled the flame which had been in his eyes when he told her to come to him. His burning gaze moved slowly, caressingly downwards, and she saw his hands clench into fists as his jaw had clenched when the robe fell.

It was absurd to feel shy when once they had been man and wife, as familiar with each other's bodies as with their own. But that was a long time ago, and she could not help flushing a little under his avid scrutiny.

"Charles, please . . . " She reached out her hands, wanting to be close to him, to be carried away by his kisses to the point where all inhibitions ceased to exist.

His hands unclenched and reached out to grasp her bare waist. He drew her against him and kissed her; his hands roving over her back from shoulder to thigh while his lips demanded and received an even more passionate response than before.

He had shaved the dark beard which had sometimes chafed her fine skin if he had neglected to do so before making love to her. While, softly, he kissed her closed eyes, she touched his newly-smooth cheeks with the tips of her fingers before delving her hands into the thick dark hair and finding its texture as pleasing as his skin and all else about him.

As his legs began nudging hers backwards until she felt the edge of the mattress behind her knees, she murmured, "Be gentle, darling. It's been so long since — "

"Haven't I always been gentle?" His deep voice was thick with desire.

"Sometimes you haven't," she whispered. She could remember nights when his lovemaking had left her as tumbled and spent as a swim in a wild winter sea. She could feel in him now the same surging force she remembered, and this was only the first wave, not the towering, all-engulfing big breaker which followed the lesser rollers and which, whenever she had watched them pounding on the rocks below her father's villa, had always been a reminder of her stormiest nights in Charles's arms.

Yet when his hold on her slackened, and he raised his head to look down at her, she did not welcome the respite but made a sound of impatience, and began to tug at his shirt which was still tucked inside his trousers.

"Why are you so over-dressed?" she whispered.

"In a moment I shan't be," he answered huskily. "Kate, will you give me your word that tomorrow you'll turn down the job?"

"What?" She couldn't believe she had heard aright.

"I don't want any misunderstanding. This is strictly for kicks. It doesn't commit us — either of us — to anything more than a few hours' enjoyment. You do understand that, I hope?"

"No," she gasped. "No — no, I don't. If you want me, take me — but don't make conditions."

"I have to. I've re-made my life, and I won't have it wrecked a second time. Either you turn down the job, or we stop this at once, here and now."

Anger blazed up inside her, but her

voice was still soft as she asked, "But can you stop, Charles?" As she spoke, she leaned lightly against him, her softness just brushing the hardness of his tanned chest, her arms twining over his shoulders, her slim hips moving incitingly.

"Yes, damn you — yes," he said roughly, wrenching her arms from his neck. "Make your choice, Katy. The job — or tonight in my arms."

She drew back. "I call that insulting!"

"Perhaps it is," he answered harshly. "But I'm not twenty-five any more, and so blindly, insanely in love with you that I couldn't even see the storm signals. I had six months of wretchedness with you, and more than a year of hell without you. I'm not such a fool as to go through all that again. A few nights together — yes, fine. But living together — impossible!"

She bent to snatch up her robe and hold it against her.

"Then you'd better go," she said unsteadily. "A quick roll in the hay is not my style, I'm afraid. I love you. I've always loved you, and if you went through hell, so did I. A worse hell, I shouldn't wonder, as I had Father's trial to cope with as well as being terribly unhappy." Her voice cracked on the last word.

"Katy — " He put out his hands, and she could see pity in his eyes.

But she didn't want his compassion and, although every nerve of her yearned to lie down with him, if the price of bliss was to end the cruise with the others, it was too high. She would not pay it. She would not be treated like one of the man-hungry passengers with whom he had sometimes amused himself in the past. It would be degrading; a travesty of the wonderful, wholehearted love they had once made together.

"Go away, Charles. Please go," she insisted, almost in tears but determined not to let him know it.

"Very well, if that's the way you want it." He began to re-button his shirt.

"Not the way I want it. The way *you* want it. I want to sleep in your arms every night for the rest of my life," she added in a low voice, her head bent over the clutched bunch of robe at her chest and her gaze fixed on her bare feet.

"That's teenage dream-world stuff, Katy. I should have thought you'd have learnt a little more realism by now."

It seemed to take him forever to do up his buttons and tuck the shirt back in his pants. When at last he was tidy, he said, "You can't take that job, and you know it. It would make life intolerable for both of us. Meanwhile there are six nights to go before the party breaks up. If you have second thoughts, let me know. I wouldn't define it as promiscuity to resume, for a few pleasant hours, the one — the only — successful side of our relationship. But anything more is out of the question."

She lifted her head, her eyes bright with unshed tears. "Then *everything* is out of the question."

Charles came a step closer and put his hand under her chin. "You may change your mind about that. Think it over: ask yourself whether life is so full of pleasure that we can afford to miss any. You're young now, and very beautiful, but you won't always be."

He pressed his mouth on her lips and, although she tried to keep them closed and unresponsive, his grip on her chin kept her face still, and she found she could not resist the practised sensuality with which he forced her to part them.

"That wasn't fair, Charles," she panted, when he let go of her chin.

"It wasn't intended to be. I hope it keeps you awake for a long time," he answered unkindly. "I've lost sleep over you often enough."

He picked up his hat, put it on and gave her an ironical salute. A moment later he had gone.

Two days later she received a message from London.

REQUIRE IMMEDIATE INSTRUCTIONS RE DISPOSAL YOUR BELONGINGS. HARCOURT.

This put Katy in a quandary. She had not yet made up her mind to defy Charles by taking the job Andreas had offered, so she could not arrange for her possessions to be sent to await the yacht's arrival in Spain. But where else could they be sent? Most of her friends lived in flats where the storage of even her few things would be an inconvenience. Robert had more space to spare, but she could no longer apply to him for assistance. Had they still been friends, she would have done. But his offer of marriage had put an end to friendship between them, and now, having met Charles again, she knew she could never be satisfied with a second-best marriage.

The only solution seemed to be to ask for her bits and pieces to be crated and put in a repository. One box should hold all she owned. Deliberately, she had eschewed acquiring too many things. Perhaps, subconsciously, she had been acting on Charles's philosophy. Unlike her father, for whom status symbols had been the principal objective in life, Charles had been apt to quote Wordsworth's lines — *The world is too much with us; late and soon, Getting and spending, we lay waste our powers.*

Some books, a transistor-cum-cassette player, a couple of paintings, a little Norwegian glass bird by Benny Motzfeldt, and one or two other small treasures were all she had now.

She had seen nothing of Charles since he had left her in her cabin with her lips inflamed by his kisses, and her emotions in the chaos resulting from mind and body at war. Her mind had been full of resentment at the arbitrary terms which she would have had to accept before he would satisfy the longings besetting her body. It had been of little comfort to guess that he, too, had spent that night in an agony of restlessness.

Much of the time Arianna and her fiancé were missing from the rest of the company, but when they were in the mood to socialise, it was usually in a foursome with Katy and David Kent.

On the day after Thalia's message had made Katy feel that, although she had until New Year's Eve, she ought not to postpone her decision until the last moment, the four of them spent the morning water-skiing. They then picnic-lunched on the beach, while the older members of the party had their lunch on board. After lunch, Arianna and Alain wandered off in search of seclusion, and Katy and David swam.

She had been renewing her sun-screen, and discussing with him the latest theories about radiodermatosis — the medical term for irreversible damage to the skin brought about by ultra-violet radiation — when, on impulse, she asked, "David, is it part of your duties to help people with all their troubles, not only their physical ones?"

"That rather depends on the nature of the trouble. I'm always ready to listen. I can't necessarily help. What's on your mind?"

"Perhaps it's unfair to burden you with my worries; but I do badly need some detached advice," she began. "You see, Andreas has invited me to spend a trial period seeing if I'm up to replacing Madame Jourdain after her retirement. I want the job very much, but Charles insists I refuse it. He says it would create an impossible situation. Is he right, do you think? Must I refuse it?"

"What about your job with Thalia Harcourt?"

Katy explained, and he said, "Mm, I guessed there was more than met the eye in her early departure. So if you do turn down the Owner's offer, you'll be out of work?"

"But not for long, I shouldn't think. I have no fears about finding another job quickly, although not one with the kudos attaching to this one."

"But it isn't the kudos which attracts you. It's being near Charles, is that right?"

"Yes, it is," she admitted. "I find I'm

as much in love with him as ever I was, and this would give me a chance to prove to him that I've changed; that I'm not the spoilt little fool who made him unhappy before. But perhaps it wouldn't be fair to force myself on him in that way. He might even be furious enough to resign his own job, and for that I could never forgive myself."

"I don't think he'd do that," said David. "He's a levelheaded chap, and he wouldn't readily resign a job which also carries great kudos in maritime circles. There was a good deal of luck involved in his getting it. He distinguished himself in a way which caught the attention of the Owner, and also he had several essential qualifications. But although he's incredibly efficient − nothing happens which he doesn't know about − in the normal way a man of Charles's age would never have reached First Officer on one of the four largest private yachts in the world. He's not going to chuck that in a hurry."

"No, that's what I think, or hope, but even so − " She finished the sentence with a shrug of uncertainty.

"Even so, I agree, it *could* be an awkward situation to have the partners in a broken marriage working in crucial positions in the tight community of a ship. It will be a good deal less awkward if nobody knows you're married except yourselves, myself, and of course the Owner."

"Andreas doesn't know yet."

"Hm, he might not take kindly to not knowing, if he found out." Katy was smoothing cream on her legs, but was aware of David's gaze resting thoughtfully on her. Presently he said, "It would seem that Charles doesn't yet share your wish for a rapprochement. Or says he doesn't. It seems to me that once or twice I've seen him looking at you in a way I shouldn't describe as hostile, or even uninterested."

"I think he still finds me . . . attractive. One can do that without liking someone."

"Oh, lord, yes. As in *Of Human Bondage* where the poor wretch couldn't resist the nasty little waitress. But your case is not like that − or am I allowing my own liking for you to cloud my judgment?" he suggested, with a smile. "I've known you for a few days, and liked everything I've discovered. But Charles has lived with you and, as the old wives say, one has to live with a person really to know them."

"He lived with me as I was, not as I am now. Do you honestly think there's very little danger of his resigning?"

"Almost nil. To be brutally frank, I think he would go to the Owner, put the position squarely to him, and ask for you to be jettisoned. And knowing how much Dracoulis likes him, I think you would be. Having said that, I think you must make up your mind without the benefit of my advice, Katy. I also like Charles very much, and I shouldn't like him to feel I'd encouraged you in a move which he deplores."

"No, you're right. It must be my decision, and I think I've already made it. But I shan't tell you, or Charles, until after I've spoken to Andreas on New Year's Eve."

Towards the end of the week between Christmas and New Year, Katy received a letter from Robert. She read it with relief, for it absolved her from feeling troubled about him.

Robert wrote that, while staying with his parents for Christmas, he had told his father about her, and whose daughter she was. His father had then revealed that his mother was not in good health and should at all cost be spared any form of anxiety.

Although Howard White's notoriety was a matter of indifference to him, Robert's letter continued, there was no doubt that it would distress his mother, an old-fashioned woman of the highest principles. He felt sure Katy would agree that to blight Mrs Otterway's last years, perhaps even to shorten them, would be selfish and wrong. Particularly as, in London, the social climate was much more relaxed than in country places, and there was no need for them to formalise their relationship until they could do so without upsetting anyone.

Writing back by return, Katy told Robert that she and Thalia had fallen out and, having been offered another job out of England, she would not be returning to London. Having had more time for reflection, she went on, she had realised that she did not wish to marry again and, although she knew she had given him the impression that an informal relationship would be acceptable to her, she felt now that it would not be. She ended her answer by thanking him for his friendship and wishing him well in the future.

As she sealed the flap of the airmail envelope and wrote his address on it, she thought it likely that when he read her reply he, too, would feel more relief than regret.

"What's become of your nice First Officer? We haven't seen him for days," said Valentina to the Captain, while she and Katy were chatting to him in the Owner's suite before dinner on the last night of the year.

"Having taught himself to speak Russian, Mr Ormond is applying himself to Arabic. He's not a man to waste time on social platitudes if he can avoid it," answered Commander Longhurst.

"Are you implying that talking to us is a waste of time? How ungallant of you, Captain," she said laughingly.

"For myself, I can't imagine a more pleasant way of spending my leisure than in conversation with two exceptionally charming members of the fair sex," he replied, with a bow.

Dracoulis passed them, and Valentina touched his arm. "You promised to show me your famous Venetian bed, Andreas. Have you seen it, Katy?"

As Katy shook her head, Dracoulis said, rather curtly, "The stories concerning my bed are largely the inventions of the press. Even its past history is open to doubt, but you're welcome to see it if it interests you."

He led the way into his bedroom which was dominated by an immense bed, the velvet-draped canopy supported by carved and painted posts.

"Which of the doges' wives did it belong to?" asked Valentina.

"It dates from the late seventeenth century, but, as I said, its provenance can be disputed. It may have been merely the bed of a prosperous merchant."

"I had an idea that a doge was a celibate, like a Pope," said Katy.

"I expect you had that impression because, for almost five hundred years, each Doge of Venice was married to the Adriatic on Ascension Day. It was a symbol of the city's sovereignty of the sea since the year 1177 when Sebastiano Liani, the Doge of the time, won a naval victory against the Emperor Frederick Barbarossa," Andreas explained.

"Afterwards, every year, the ceremonial marriage took place on a state galley called *Bucentaur.* The last of the galleys was built in the 1720s, and burned by the French just before the end of the century. But the Doge was a chief magistrate, not a potentate of the Church. The history of Venice in her heyday is very enthralling. I have always felt I should have enjoyed living then and, when this bed was offered to me, I bought it."

The First Officer did join the rest of them for dinner, and Katy wondered if he would still be present at midnight, and would take advantage of the occasion to kiss her.

Immediately after dinner Andreas sought her out and, drawing her a little aside, asked, "Have you made up your mind, Katy?"

"Yes, I have. I should like to see if I can measure up to the job."

"Splendid. We'll discuss the practicalities tomorrow. For the present you are still my guest, and I want to dance with you."

Shortly before twelve o'clock, stewards circulated with yet more champagne and, on the first stroke of midnight, their host raised his glass to toast the New Year.

There was an outbreak of kissing and good wishes, and David, who was standing next to Katy, said, "May I?" and kissed her cheek.

She saw Charles approaching, a predatory gleam in his eyes. Whether he would have kissed her she was never to know. She put out her hand so that he would be forced to shake it before attempting a less formal salutation.

She said, "Happy New Year. I have some news for you both. I'm not leaving with the others the day after tomorrow. I'm joining the crew as assistant to Madame Jourdain."

"We shall enjoy having you with us," said David.

Probably involuntarily, for she knew he was careful with his grip when shaking hands with women, Charles's fingers tightened painfully hard upon hers.

"Happy New Year," he said curtly. He remembered to give the doctor a friendly clap on the shoulder before he turned away, but he could not conceal the flash of rage in his eyes.

When she was the only one left of the Christmas guests, Katy found she saw little of her husband. Andreas had insisted that, for the time being, she should remain in the cabin she had occupied during the cruise. She had her meals with Madame Jourdain. The officers ate in their ward-room. While still in Caribbean waters she continued to use the pool, and to chat to David and the Captain when they were there at the same time as herself. But Charles never was, and she knew this could not be coincidence. He was avoiding her. Half way across the Atlantic they ran into a violent storm which was her first experience of bad weather. During the months she had spent on board Charles's sloop there had never been more than a fresh breeze and a slight swell, so she had no means of knowing how good a sailor she was.

Madame Jourdain was a bad sailor who, forewarned of what lay ahead, took pills and retired to her quarters to remain lying down until it was over.

"If you feel ill, you must do the same,"

she advised Katy. "It is foolish to try to fight seasickness. It's not very often that we experience bad weather, and never with passengers on board."

However, when they entered the storm zone and, for eighteen hours, were rolling and pitching to an extent which prostrated a number of people besides Madame Jourdain, Katy found herself unaffected. Indeed the raging elements seemed an exciting change from the unvarying calm of the voyage so far. Had it not been for the distress caused to others, she would have enjoyed the wild weather.

It was during the storm that she had one of her rare encounters with the First Officer. On one of his tours of inspection, he entered one of the pantry galleys to find her with a mug of tea in one hand and a cold beef sandwich in the other.

"Not laid low, Miss Brown?" he remarked, with a lifted eyebrow.

"Not at all low," she answered cheerfully, unable to help feeling pleased with herself, although she knew — Charles having told her — that there was no personal credit in not being ill in rough seas.

He himself, on his round-the-world

voyage, had several times been very ill. Now, having seen other people in the throes of acute seasickness, she realised, more vividly than before, what it must be like to have been alone in conditions even more ferocious than those which *Artemis* were experiencing. Her admiration for the courage of all single-handed circum-navigators, and particularly for his, had increased four-fold since seeing for herself the huge mid-ocean waves on which the great yacht was riding.

"Good girl," was his comment and, for an instant, she thought she saw in his eyes a glimmer of the approving looks he had used to give her long ago, at the very beginning of their relationship.

But perhaps she had only imagined it, she thought, as she finished her sandwich. 'Good girl' probably meant no more than 'Well done' or 'Keep it up' or any of the encouraging phrases used by those in command to those under them in times of stress.

However, although not at any time affected by queasiness, she did not survive the storm unscathed. During one particularly violent pitch, she was flung off her feet and, in falling, bashed her side with a force which made her hiss with pain.

The next day she was badly bruised, and it hurt her to move her arm, but she managed to conceal this from anyone's notice. However, the following day the pain seemed worse rather than better, and the housekeeper, catching sight of an uncontrollable wince, made Katy admit what had happened, and sent her to the sick bay.

The door of Doctor Kent's office was ajar. She tapped and entered at the same moment that he emerged from an inner door which she knew led to his operating theatre.

"Hello, Katy. What can I do for you?" As he spoke, he went into his dispensary and she heard him unlocking a cupboard.

Raising her voice, she explained,

"Madame Jourdain insisted I come to you. I slipped and fell during the storm, and she thinks I may have cracked a rib. I'm quite sure I haven't, but she insists I have a check-up."

"Does it hurt when you breathe?"

"A little, but that could be bruising."

David reappeared with a box in his hand.

"I think you'd better have an X-ray. I can't do it now, I'm afraid, I've a chap in there with a smashed hand. Can you come back at, say, six o'clock?"

"Yes, of course."

"I could X-ray Miss Brown for you, David," a voice said from behind her.

She turned and saw Charles in the doorway.

The young doctor hesitated briefly, before saying, "Yes, you know the drill, don't you, Charles. Would you have any objection to the First Officer attending to you, Katy?"

"Why should she?" Charles enquired coolly. "You get on with repairing Seaman Parker's hand, David, and I'll do my stuff with the X-ray machine. This way . . . Miss Brown."

Rather uncertainly, Katy followed him to the X-ray room.

"When did you fall?" he enquired, shutting the door and enclosing them in the small room which housed the X-ray equipment.

"Two days ago, but I'm sure it's not serious. I'm only here to please Madame."

"You were foolish not to report it

immediately. Take off your shirt, will you, please?"

He said this without glancing at her, his attention on his preparations. But when, after some moments, she had not obeyed the instruction, he added, "No one else will come in. There's a warning light outside the door when this room is in use."

It had not been the thought of being seen undressed by someone else which had caused her to hesitate. Under her white cotton top she was wearing a tan seamless bra which covered as much, if not more, as the tops of any of her bikinis. It was because he was there that she did not want to undress. Had David or a medical orderly been X-raying her, she would have complied without hesitation.

"Show me where you hurt yourself," he said, when her shirt was off.

Cautiously, Katy raised her left arm and, with her other hand, indicated the area which was painful.

"There isn't much visible bruising," he said. "I think you'd better strip off completely. The metal bits on a bra can interfere with the picture."

"Is — is there one of those cotton triangles?"

"What cotton triangles?"

"For women to wear for being X-rayed."

"As we're dealing with men most of the time, I imagine that's one piece of equipment we haven't got. I shouldn't think many women would want one, considering how much of themselves they expose on the pool deck." As she continued to hesitate, he went on impatiently, "Is this modesty really necessary? I have seen you undressed before. I believe I shall be able to restrain myself from behaving unethically."

Vexed by his sarcastic tone, and even more annoyed with herself for blushing, she unclipped the bra and removed it.

To give him his due, his manner from then on was as impersonal as if he were a professional radiologist. But she was acutely aware that he wasn't; he was a man before whom, in the past, she had never once taken off her clothes without his wanting to touch her, not always with the intention of making love to her, but for the pleasure it gave him to run a possessive hand over her body. She could not believe that now, in spite of his outward indifference, he did not want to stroke her, and the memory of past caresses made her quiver suddenly. She felt sure he noticed the movement and guessed its cause, and her skin seemed to burn with her chagrin that, while he appeared unaffected, she could not hide her reactions.

She was thankful when she had finished, and she could dress herself. As she was standing with her back to him, fumbling with the clip of her bra because it was painful to put her left hand behind her but she could not manage with one hand, he said, "Let me do that for you," making her jump at finding him so close behind her.

As he took the two ends of the band, his knuckles brushed against her skin. "Which slot?"

"The inner one, please. Thank you."

As she reached for her shirt, he said, "Let's hope my efforts are successful, or we may have to repeat the process, and you wouldn't like that, would you, Katy?"

"No doubt Dr Kent will be free to take a second lot if there's anything wrong with those you've done."

"And you don't mind undressing for

him, but you do for me, mm?"

"I used not to, but now that you seem to regard me only as . . . as a sex object, I don't much care for it," she agreed crisply.

"Little liar. You were disappointed that I behaved so impeccably — "

As she turned angrily to deny this, he went on, "Although, naturally, you won't admit it. But your sex never really mind a man getting out of line. It's the absence of reaction which peeves them, as was proved by the Harcourt woman."

"What an arrant piece of male-thinking nonsense!" she retorted indignantly. "If you hadn't behaved impeccably I should have been furious."

"Another black lie, my dear Katy. You wanted my hands on your breasts just as much as I wanted them there — which I admit readily. Not to touch you more than was necessary was quite an effort, believe me. So why not stop all this shilly-shallying and — when your side has stopped hurting — give me what I want, and what you want too, if you're honest."

"I've told you why not, several times. The only way you will ever get me into bed with you is as Katy Ormond."

"You're Katy Ormond now."

"Not publicly, and I don't care for being thought to be the First Officer's current popsie. It would be bad for my relations with the stewardesses and the other crew."

Without waiting for his answer, she left the room.

But it was not the last she was to see of him that day. About nine o'clock, when she was reading in her cabin, she called 'Come in' in response to a knock at the door, and was startled and discomposed when it was her husband who entered.

"What do you want?" she asked sharply.

"Relax, Kate," he answered dryly. "David sent me to tell you the X-rays show no serious damage, and to give you some ointment which should ease the soreness you're feeling."

"Oh, I see . . . thank you."

"If you'd like to lie down, I'll apply some."

It was her turn to speak dryly. "I'm sure he didn't suggest that."

"He knows we are, or were, married. That's why he allowed me to do your X-ray."

"Yes, he guessed it some time ago, and I saw no reason not to admit he was right."

"And to enlist him as your advocate," he remarked sardonically.

"Is he? I didn't know. I think he likes me — I hope so. And doctors are usually good judges of people, shouldn't you think?"

"Older, more experienced ones, probably. David is a clever medico. I don't think he knows much about women on a non-medical level."

"How much do you know about them? Oh, yes, a great deal about how to please them in bed, but perhaps not very much else. You made a bad choice of a wife, and having committed one mistake, you didn't know how to retrieve it — as I think other men would have done when the wife was as young and malleable as I was in those days. You could have made what you liked of me, but you wanted perfection ready-made, and now that life has re-made me, you refuse to see it."

To her horror, she burst into tears at the very same moment that someone else knocked at the door.

Before she had regained enough control of herself to tell Charles not to answer it, he had moved to the door and opened it, but not so wide that whoever was standing outside could see Katy hurriedly mopping her eyes with a tissue.

"Ah, Madame Jourdain," he said, sounding relieved. "I've just been telling Miss Brown that her ribs are in excellent order, apart from some bruising for which Dr Kent has prescribed an ointment. She may need some help to apply it. I'll leave her in your care."

Having stood aside to allow the Frenchwoman to enter, he left the cabin and closed the door.

If Madame noticed that her assistant's lashes were wet and her manner strained, she pretended not to; nor did she argue with Katy's assurance that she did not need help with the ointment. Having expressed her relief that the X-ray had shown no rib damage, she went away.

The rest of the voyage was comparatively calm. They berthed briefly at Las Palmas in the Canaries, then continued north towards Gibraltar which they passed in the night. The first Katy saw of Spain, the country of her marriage, was when she looked out of the port and saw the rugged sierras behind the part of the coast where Andreas was building what he called his answer to Monaco.

The weather, although not as idyllic as that in the West Indies, was sunny and warm by day but cool after darkness had fallen. Although she and Charles had swum in the Mediterranean in winter, compared with the Caribbean the sea in Spain felt very cold, but Katy continued to use the now heated pool.

The Owner rejoined *Artemis* two days after her arrival. It was early afternoon when Katy, leaving the pool deck after her lunch break, saw a large silver Mercedes gliding slowly along the quay of the newly constructed deep water berth where the yacht was lying.

She had not expected to have any contact with Andreas until the following day, if then. So she was surprised when, within an hour of his arrival, she received a note from him bidding her to have dinner with him in his suite.

He opened the door to her himself and,

having shaken her hand, he tucked it inside his elbow and led her into the study and across the room to the corner where two right-angled sofas formed a comfortable sitting area.

"How are you, Katy? You had a rough time coming over, but you proved yourself an excellent sailor, I'm told."

He himself mixed their pre-dinner drinks, introducing her to a Persian drink called a Golnar which had a vodka base — the only spirit, so he said, to drink before and after wine — to which he added ice and a dash of cherry brandy before topping it up with pomegranate juice.

The meal, as always, was delicious; beginning with a mousse of avocado and smoked salmon, followed by chicken breasts garnished with mushrooms and asparagus tips.

While they ate, Andreas talked not of the Spanish project, the progress of which he had come to inspect, but of the new plans in his mind. Yet although she was conscious of being in the presence of genius, he did not intimidate her as Charles did. But perhaps that was only because, in Charles's eyes, she was still the immature Katy of four years ago.

It was not until dinner was over, and they had returned to the sofa corner for coffee, that Andreas said, "Have you found life on board congenial? Would you like to continue to make *Artemis* your home?"

"I should like it very much, but I don't know whether Madame Jourdain considers me fit to succeed her."

"She considers you more than equal to it. But in fact if you do stay on board it will not be in the capacity of housekeeper. I'm afraid I misled you, my dear. It has never been my intention to employ you. I should like you to become my wife."

There was a long pause, at the end of which Katy said softly, "You can't be serious!"

"Why not? Does the difference in our ages seem an insuperable gulf to you? Do I seem far too old, and short, and grey-haired to be acceptable as a lover to someone as young and beautiful as yourself?"

"No, no — of course not," she answered. "You know you're very attractive, and will be in twenty years' time. Some men always are, all their lives. But . . . I'm not in love with you, Andreas."

"I know that. It has no bearing on my suggestion. I'm not proposing a love match. As I think I mentioned some time ago, I want to have several more children, and you told me you'd like six. That would be the foundation of our marriage, and on it I think we could build a very comfortable relationship."

He paused to light a cigar before he continued, "I had marriage in mind before I left, but I felt a period of separation and reflection was advisable. As soon as I saw you again, and had talked to you for ten minutes, I knew my plan was a sound one. You have all the qualities I require in my fourth and last wife; and, although I may not be the man of whom you have dreamed, I believe as a real-life husband I should not prove unsatisfactory."

"Andreas, you hardly know me. You don't even know my real name. It isn't Brown. I adopted that name to make life easier for myself after my father was sent to prison."

Although Howard White's trial had made headlines in England, she did not expect it to have made much impression, if any, on the Greek millionaire by whose standards her father's activities had been small beer.

Her eyes fixed on her tightly clasped hands, she recounted the charges on which her father had been found guilty and imprisoned. When, having come to the end, she looked at Andreas again, his expression showed neither surprise nor displeasure.

"My dear child, I have been guilty of a far worse crime than your father," he said heavily. "Oh, not one for which I could be imprisoned, but it lies very heavily on my conscience."

"What do you mean?"

"One of my earliest enterprises," said Andreas, "was to supply the livers of sharks and whales to a pharmaceutical company for the manufacture of Vitamin A tablets. In those days I had only two vessels involved in the slaughter, but later I built up a large whaling fleet. That whales are now in serious danger of extinction is, in part, due to my activities. To help to stamp out a species is a crime as horrible as genocide, particularly now that scientists are building up evidence which shows that whales and dolphins have a culture far older, and probably far superior, to that of men. Have you read about the latest discoveries?"

Katy shook her head. She could see that he was sincere when he spoke of his feeling of guilt.

He went on, "They are fascinating: to me, far more exciting than our quests into space. Did you know that a humpback whale can produce a 'symphony' lasting for as long as half an hour, and which another whale, hearing it for the first time, can repeat perfectly? They're thought to have brains capable of dealing with problems far more complex than those which the human mind can handle."

Where, moments ago, his dark brown eyes had been sombre, now they were alight with enthusiasm. "You know the slogan — Make love, not war. It may be that whales have had that idea for thirty million years. Think what they could teach us if only we could learn to communicate with them! That's why I consider your father's offences trivial compared with my own. Already one of the laws which he broke has been revoked, and bribery is surely a venial sin, not a mortal one?"

"Perhaps, but nevertheless a great many people would shun me if they knew I was his daughter."

"They would have better grounds for shunning me," said Andreas with a wry grimace. There was a pause before he added, "There's something else you want to tell me, I think?"

There was, but she could not confess her other secret because it was not hers alone, and she had no right to reveal what Charles might prefer to conceal. In any case, her married status would have been relevant only if she had wanted to become the fourth Madame Dracoulis.

She said, "Only that I'm very flattered at being asked, but I can't accept your proposal. I'm sure that a marriage based on practical considerations can work out very well in some cases, but it wouldn't do for me, Andreas."

"Don't say no immediately. Think it over as I did. You once told me you had reason to know that beauty alone was not enough to hold the kind of man you wanted. Am I right in concluding there's been an important but unsuccessful love affair in your life?"

"Yes — a love I've never got over, and perhaps never will," she admitted.

"Never is a long time, and you're still very young. What went wrong? Was he married already?"

"No . . . nothing like that. It just fell apart in much the same way, I suppose, as your second and third marriages."

"I didn't expect them to last. My last wife and the one before her were interested only in my money, and for me they were merely playthings — pretty toys who very soon ceased to amuse me."

"If you knew that, why did you marry them?"

"Because in my earlier years certain women could make me feel I had to possess them. Don't think me offensive if I say that most women have a price which I have the good fortune — maybe it is a misfortune — of being able to pay. These two were astute enough not to settle for a few jewels and furs. Virtue was its own reward — although not in the usual meaning of that expression."

"Didn't you mind? Knowing that they didn't love you?"

"No. My first wife, Artemis, loved me, and I knew I couldn't expect to repeat my happiness with her. One has to be realistic. Few people are blessed with all the gifts of the gods. Health, beauty, talent, money — the prizes are many. But one can't expect to win every one of them." He leaned over to clasp her hands. "You have youth, and a lovely face. I can give you a life in the sun, luxury, children, contentment. Might that not be better than pining for the man who made you unhappy?"

Katy looked down at the hands holding hers; the strong, short-fingered hands of a peasant or a fisherman, but without the callouses and broken nails. She remembered now, at the beginning of the Christmas cruise, she had thought that if Charles did not exist she could have fallen in love with Andreas. But Charles did exist, his presence haunting her continually so that even now, while one of the world's richest men was offering to share his wealth with her, she was comparing his stubby fingers with the long lean fingers which had only to touch her cheek in the lightest caress to send a thrill through her.

"I think it would be much better," said Andreas, answering the question for her. "But, as I say, think it over, as you did when I offered you a job."

It was clear to her that, however many times she reiterated her refusal now, he was not going to be convinced until, as he suggested, she had thought it over.

Although he made no further reference to marriage, in the next few days Andreas engaged in a form of discreet courtship. He insisted she had breakfast with him, and lunch, and in the evenings they dined together. But although he exerted the full force of his very engaging personality on her, it was always from the other side of the table or across the distance between the two sofas. He never attempted to make even mild love to her and, after the first evening alone with him, when they said goodnight at half past ten, she did not spend any more evenings uneasily conscious of the famous bed in the inner room.

Although he pooh-poohed her concern that the rest of the ship might be speculating about her relationship with him, Katy felt sure that, however discreet the steward might be, he was not the only one privy to the fact of their eating together. The galley staff must know too.

"There is nothing I can keep secret from my steward and my valet," said Andreas easily. "They know there is nothing between us worthy of gossip, and the others will take their word for it."

But in that he was wrong. The next day, while Andreas was busy ashore and her lunch consisted of yoghurt and an apple on the pool deck, Charles came to her and said abruptly, "The day I X-rayed your ribs, you told me you didn't want to be known as my popsie because it would undermine your staff relations."

"Yes, I remember," she said stiffly.

"I think you should know," he went on, "that the crew are beginning to gossip about your relationship with Dracoulis. It's obvious his interest in you goes beyond your present position."

"They're right. It does," she agreed calmly.

"For God's sake, Katy, don't you know the kind of man he is? He got rid of two wives when he tired of them. Do you want to be known as *his* popsie? And, later, as one of his cast-offs?"

"No, I should dislike it very much. But that possibility doesn't arise. I trust you to keep it to yourself, Charles, but the fact is that Andreas has asked me to marry him."

She had wanted to take the wind out of his sails, and she had succeeded.

"My God! That hadn't occurred to me," he said, his tone incredulous. Then, recovering himself, "That's quite an achievement. So now, of course, you want your freedom?"

Katy stared at him. Clearly it didn't even cross his mind that she might have refused the millionaire's offer of marriage. Before she could tell him she had, Charles went on, "You can have it. I shan't stand in your way." He paused. "But there is one condition . . . "

Her curiosity pricked, she said, "What condition?"

He did not reply immediately, but stared down at her with a strange, hot glitter in his usually cold eyes. "You've given me good times and bad times, Katy — recently some very bad times. Before we separate legally and finally, I'd like to have one more good time. You can marry Dracoulis if that's what you want. But before you do, I want one last night in your bed . . . 'one night of love', as the song says."

6

"THAT's a monstrous suggestion!" she whispered, aghast.

"Is it? Why? If you can contemplate sleeping for years with a man you don't love, I fail to see why you should jib at a single night with one whom, only quite recently, you professed to love," he said cruelly.

She was on the point of telling him that, unbelievable as he might find it, she meant to refuse Andreas, when something in her seemed to snap.

It was as if the shock of meeting him again, followed by the several emotional scenes which had taken place between them since, had stretched her nerves tighter and tighter until the strain had reached its limit and left her incapable of coping with any further stress. She found herself thinking: Oh, to hell with it. Why not?

With a deep sigh of nervous exhaustion, she said, "Very well. You win, Charles."

He looked, she thought, somewhat

surprised. She felt a kind of bitter amusement, bordering on hysteria.

"When do you suggest? And where? Your cabin or mine?" she asked recklessly.

"I'll come to your cabin tonight." He turned on his heel and walked away.

Katy watched him go, then closed her eyes and lay back on the lounger where he had found her. How very restful life was if one abandoned all moral scruples and principles and became a hedonist, she thought. Perhaps, after all, she did take after her father and, in withstanding Charles so far, had been fighting against her true nature. It might even be that, having previously regarded Carly and Thalia and their like as rather abandoned and sinful, she was on the brink of joining them.

She remembered David Kent warning her that if, at that time, Charles had asked Andreas to choose between them, probably the Owner would have chosen to get rid of her. But would he now? She thought not. Yet the knowledge that it was in her power to revenge herself against Charles for his merciless treatment gave her no satisfaction.

As she went about her tasks that afternoon,

she made up her mind that, as soon as Andreas came back on board, she would tell him she could not marry him and that she would like to leave the yacht the following morning. She thought she might go to Paris and try to find work there. French and German had been her best subjects at school. Her German was rusty, but she had kept up her French.

However, this intention was frustrated by the fact that when Andreas returned to the yacht he was accompanied by several men, and later he telephoned Katy in her cabin to explain that he would be occupied that evening but would like her to breakfast with him as usual the following morning.

It was a nerve-racking evening. She had no idea what time Charles would come to her, so she dared not tackle her packing in case he arrived before she had finished and hidden the cases in the wardrobe, and demanded to know why she was doing it.

She knew she could go through with the night ahead only if he thought she was under duress. She could not bear him to discover, before she had gone, that she had capitulated because she wished to, because she could not face the future without one last bitter-sweet memory and, even now, could not quite give up hope that the act of love would change his mind.

Somehow — she wasn't sure how — she had to make it the most wonderful, unforgettable night he had ever spent with a woman. As everything she knew about love had been taught her by Charles, she could only hope that being older, and having suffered great heartache, would make a difference.

Although she had not been a timid bride and had never resisted his caresses, she seemed to recall that in the short time of their marriage she had sometimes felt shy of acting on all her own impulses. But tonight, when he came to her, she meant to abandon all restraints, except in speech. However far gone in passion, she would not tell him in words how greatly she loved him.

It took her some time to decide whether to be clothed or unclothed when he arrived. Would it please him more to undress her, or to find her already naked?

In the end, when at last he came, the cabin was lit only by the two shafts of moonlight streaming through the ports, and Katy was curled in the chair, wearing only a fine gold chain at the base of her throat, and drinking a glass of chilled white wine which, because she had been quite unable to eat any dinner, had already gone to her head slightly.

For an instant she saw his tall frame silhouetted by the light from outside, and then the door closed behind him and he leaned against it, his tanned face a dark, inscrutable mask above the whiteness of his uniform.

She swallowed the rest of the wine, uncoiled slim bare legs and, with one lithe movement, stood up. Without a word she stepped into a pool of moonlight and slowly revolved, her hands going up to her hair to pile it on top of her head and then let it fall.

She would have revolved a second time, but Charles lunged away from the door and snatched her into his arms, with a sound like a growl.

His first kiss was fierce and punitive, his mouth grinding down on hers, his hands spreading over her shoulder-blades to hold her against him, and then, when he found her unresisting, sliding down the smooth arc of her back to grip her soft flanks and make her tremblingly aware how urgently he wanted her.

Remembering how long it had been since their bodies had joined, she felt a sharp stab of fear. In this mood of savage impatience he could hurt her more now than he had when she was a virgin and he had been skilful and tender, yet unable to spare her one instant of rending agony.

But her cowardice was only momentary. Let him hurt her, if that would relieve him of four years of pent-up bitterness.

Charles picked her up. In two strides he was by the bed where he let her fall with a roughness which made her gasp. She lay, spreadeagled and wide-eyed, while swiftly he stripped off his clothes.

His shirt went first, tossed aside to reveal the magnificent shoulders. Then he ripped down the zip of his trousers and she glimpsed his long, hard-muscled thighs as he took them off. His underpants, shoes and socks followed. Then his wrist-watch, as if he had sensed her moment of panic and, in spite of his own raging desire, it pleased him to prolong her suspense.

At this point she closed her eyes, forcing

herself to disobey the natural instinct to brace her body against his onslaught and, instead, to relax and yield. With a tremor, she felt the mattress give under his weight, and saw his dark shape poised to swoop. Then his hands clamped down on her arms, a hard knee was thrust between hers, and she knew herself to be inescapably pinioned.

When she woke and peered at the clock it was two o'clock in the morning and, beside her, Charles was asleep, lying sprawled on his back in the centre of the bed while she occupied a scant third of it.

Raising herself on one elbow, she began, very softly, to caress him, running feather-light fingertips over the planes of his now relaxed body. He had not hurt her at all; at least not in any physical way. Perhaps he had meant to take her swiftly and brutally, but when it came to the point he was as incapable of making love badly as of mishandling a boat. Although, afterwards, she had cried, it was not from any hurt he had inflicted on her bodily, or because he had left her awake when he went to sleep. The tears which had coursed down her cheeks had been caused only by his failure to say what she had hoped he might have been compelled to admit. *I want you. Forget Andreas. Come back to me. You're mine. You've always been mine.*

Now, in the middle of the night — this short night which was her last chance to rekindle the love he had felt for her once — she began to make love to him. Presently, although his eyes remained closed, she knew he was no longer sleeping and, at any moment, the outflung arms would close round her.

Even though she had been waiting for it, when suddenly he seized her and rolled her on to her back, he made her gasp and, just for an instant, resist his imprisoning arms. Then his mouth came down in a kiss which drove every thought from her mind until, with his lips near her ear, he whispered harshly, "Remember this when you're in bed with Dracoulis."

The taunt made her struggle to free herself, but he held her down with the arm which was under her shoulders, and with another long kiss which pressed her head into the pillow. She squirmed, and her hands which, before, had been caressing his head and the back of his neck became small clenched fists which pounded angrily but unavailingly on his shoulders as his free hand stroked a slow path from her throat to her thighs.

In those moments she felt she hated him; for using his superior strength, for thinking so poorly of her, and for knowing so well how to overcome her resistance until no more force was necessary, until she was once more enslaved by the languorous pleasure of feeling his strong, sure hands roving freely over her body, and the drug-like effect of his kisses.

Not once, but again and again, he forced her to the brink of ecstasy and then, so it seemed, held her back from the ultimate frenzy which would, at least partially, have released her from the hypnotic power he had over her.

She found herself gasping his name, aching to murmur the words she longed both to say and to hear. But although she could feel his heart pounding, and guessed it was not easy for him to leash his own ardour, at the same time it seemed to amuse him to postpone his final possession and, between each long burning kiss, to watch her shuddering and writhing in the throes of his sweet, expert torment.

The next time she surfaced from sleep, she was immediately conscious of the forgotten well-being of waking up after a night of love. But the deep-seated sense of happiness and peace did not last very long. Almost immediately she realised the bed was all hers: Charles had gone.

It was just growing light. For a long time she lay in a trance of despair at the failure of her last desperate attempt to retrieve the happiness lost four years ago. Without Charles the future seemed hardly worth living. She wished she had died in his arms, for what was the point of going on when she knew now, beyond any doubt, that no one else could take his place, ever.

In that case why not marry Andreas? At least you could be miserable in comfort, an inner voice seemed to suggest. But Katy knew now that even that recourse was barred to her. She could not endure any further contact with Charles, and neither did she want to disrupt his career on *Artemis.* There was nothing for it but to leave the yacht, resume her own career, and hope that, eventually, the pain she was feeling would subside to a bearable level as it had before. At least she had the comfort of knowing that Charles was alive and making a success of his life, not drifting in the South Seas, letting his abilities go to waste because of what she had done to him.

After a while she got up, bathed, and began to pack. It seemed a long time since that late December day in London when, full of excited anticipation, she had filled the cases with her cruise clothes, never dreaming how much her life would have changed before she returned to northern Europe.

When she joined Andreas for breakfast, he apologised for neglecting her the day before, and planned to make up for it today, perhaps by taking her to meet some friends who had a beautiful villa high up in the hills behind the coast.

He seemed not to notice the uncertainty of Katy's response, or her lack of appetite. It was not until he had satisfied his own hearty appetite that she found the courage to begin her confession.

"Andreas, I haven't been honest with you, and now I must be — and you'll be angry, I'm afraid."

"Angry with you? I doubt that. In what way have you deceived me?" he asked, with an encouraging smile.

"I — I didn't tell you that the man I loved — and still do love — was here, on board *Artemis*." The little Greek's smiling look faded into gravity.

"He . . . he is your First Officer," she went on, in a low voice.

"Ormond? You love Charles Ormond?"

"I was his wife. We separated four years ago. It was a great shock to meet him again, that first night in the Caribbean. I didn't say anything because it didn't seem to concern anyone but ourselves. I had told Thalia who my father was, but not about my broken marriage. I didn't foresee that Charles would be the only man who would take her fancy, and that my failure to confide in her would lead to another break-up, between her and me. Nor did I dream that you would ask me to marry you. I should have said then that, legally, I wasn't free. But I was so mixed up, and still am. Only two things are quite clear now.

281

One is that I shall never marry again."

"And the second?"

"That it's useless to go on trying to patch up my first marriage. So I have to leave . . . now, today."

Having listened to these revelations without any visible signs of amazement, he gave her a long, thoughtful look. At length he said, "Something has happened since I saw you yesterday. I mean between you and Ormond."

"Yes, we've had a . . . a sort of showdown, and I've accepted at last that there's no place for me in the new life he's made since we parted. I had hoped we might be reconciled, but no — it isn't to be," she said dully.

"Does he know I have asked you to marry me?"

"Yes. Immediately he offered me my freedom. There was a time when he would have refused it, but not any more."

"You say you wish to leave at once. Where will you go?"

"I thought I'd try Paris."

"You have friends there?"

She shook her head. "But my French is quite good."

"What about funds?"

She had not thought about money. With dismay she realised that what she had with her might be enough to cover her rail fare to Paris, and a couple of nights in a cheap *pension*, but not more. Most of her savings were invested, and it might take a little time to have the money she had in her bank in London transferred to a bank in Paris.

Andreas saw her concern, and said, "Even if you feel you can't marry me, there's no reason why we shouldn't remain friends, my dear. Please allow me to come to your aid until you have found your feet again. In Paris I have a comfortable little pied-à-terre. You are more than welcome to use it as your base while you look for a job and a place to live. I'll arrange your flight for you, and warn my caretaker when to expect you."

"It's terribly kind of you, Andreas. I will stay in your flat, most gratefully, for a night or two; but I won't fly to Paris. I'll go by train."

"Out of the question," he said dismissively. "Even a first-class private compartment would be far from comfortable on so long a journey, besides being a great waste of time. You will fly and, if you must, repay me when you can do so conveniently. Now I think you should finish your packing. I believe there's a flight from Malaga to Madrid about eleven o'clock."

Before noon Katy was high in the sky above the mountains of southern Spain, having parted from Andreas at the airport. He had insisted in seeing her off in person. Katy wondered if, from somewhere on one of the upper decks, Charles had seen her and his employer getting into the car together, not realising at the time that her luggage was in the boot and it was the last he would see of her. He would not find that out until later.

Her flight from Madrid to Paris was delayed by several hours, and it was late in the evening when she arrived at the luxurious apartment in the heart of the French capital which Andreas said he made use of for only a few days each year.

There were no living-in staff, and the woman who looked after the place went home within an hour of Katy's arrival. She had provided a cold supper which Katy ate from a tray, watching television in an effort to stop herself thinking of the night before, or of the long, loveless years which now stretched ahead of her like a desert.

She had eaten as much as she could manage when the telephone rang. It was Andreas, calling to enquire about her journey.

"I don't like to think of you being in Paris on your own. You should have someone to look after you," he remarked presently.

"I feel very well looked after, being in this lovely flat instead of in an impersonal room in an hotel. You've been wonderfully forbearing about all this," was her answer.

She longed to ask if he had seen anything of Charles since her departure, and if her husband now knew she had gone. If Andreas had said nothing to him, perhaps Madame Jourdain would have mentioned it. Katy had felt it would have been unforgivably discourteous to leave the yacht without saying goodbye to her. She had not explained to the Frenchwoman why she no longer wanted to replace her when she retired, nor had the housekeeper asked, although she must have felt considerable curiosity.

"I'll call you again in the morning. If you are still of the same mind, I'll put you in touch with a woman who lives in Paris and can be of assistance to you," he said. Then he repeated the last thing he had said to her before she boarded the plane. "That you have turned me down as a husband is no reason to deny me the pleasure of befriending you."

He added, "You are a rarity in my life, Katy — a beautiful young woman with no ulterior motive for making herself pleasant to me. Goodnight, my dear."

At one o'clock in the morning, when she was still awake, the sound of the buzzer startled her. For a moment or two she couldn't think what the noise was. Then she remembered the caretaker telling her that, although there was a porter on duty downstairs from early morning to mid-evening, at night callers at the flats had to announce themselves on a speaker-phone outside the electrically-operated main door which, when the porter was off duty, could be opened only by press buttons inside the flats.

Thinking that whoever had their finger

on the buzzer must be pressing the wrong button, and would presently realise their mistake, Katy lay waiting for the sound to cease. But when it did not after perhaps a full minute of continuous buzzing, she couldn't stand it any longer and switched on the light. The speaker-phone in the outer hall was part of the intercom system connecting all the rooms in the apartment, including the bathrooms. With the receiver of the house telephone to her ear, she said curtly, "Who is it?" — half expecting the reply to be uttered in the slurred accents of someone who had had too much to drink.

But the voice which answered was as sharply impatient as her own had been.

"Katy? It's Charles. Open the door, will you, please."

Although courteously phrased, it was an order rather than a request.

Charles here in Paris! How could he be? she thought, in startled bewilderment.

"W-what do you want?" she stammered.

"I have to talk to you."

"At this hour? Do you realise what time it is?" she asked, playing for time in which to pull herself together.

"Eight minutes past one. You've been up later," was the brisk answer. "Come on, open up."

"Why can't we talk in the morning?"

"Because I want to talk now. You have my word I shan't touch you."

She hesitated. Charles could only know where she was because Andreas had told him. Why had the Greek allowed him to follow her to Paris? Was it possible that, in a misguided attempt to play fairy godfather and grant her dearest wish, Andreas had put pressure on Charles to make things up with her? No, it couldn't be that; much as he valued his position on *Artemis* and the prospects which went with it, Charles would never yield to that kind of coercion.

"Very well — if you insist." She pressed the button which operated the doors downstairs.

In the few minutes' grace while he crossed the lobby and used the lift, she put on a dressing-gown and slippers and went to the bathroom hurriedly to splash her face with cold water and tidy her hair. Her hand shook as she used a spiral brush to smooth out the tangles caused by her restlessness since going to bed.

The bell rang before she was ready and, although she had been expecting it, her nerves were so taut that she jumped. When she opened the door Charles strode in, dumping a large canvas grip on the floor before shedding a light-coloured Burberry windcheater under which he was wearing a navy blue guernsey he had owned but seldom worn in Spain, and a pair of fawn corduroy pants which she did not recognise. It was strange to see him in civilian clothes again, but they did not make him look any less formidable than he had in the uniform of First Officer.

Clearly he was in a towering rage, but had it under control — at least for the moment.

"Why did you lie to me?" he demanded.

"L-lie to you? What about?"

"You made me believe you intended to marry Dracoulis."

"I said he'd asked me. I never said I'd accepted."

She turned to move further away from him, but before she had taken two steps he caught her by the shoulder and swung her to face him.

"But you knew very well I thought you had. You didn't correct my misapprehension."

"Five minutes ago you promised you wouldn't touch me," she reminded him, meeting his angry eyes with outward self-possession and inward agitation.

He dropped his hand, but he did not step back. "You must know I should never have forced those terms on you if I hadn't believed you meant to sell yourself to him."

She said coolly, "You underestimate him, you know. Without his money, Andreas would still attract women by the force of his personality . . . and by his kindness. No one would call you a kind man, Charles. Some people would call you a cruel one for what you did to me last night. The fact that I wasn't unwilling doesn't really excuse your behaviour. To take a woman without any warm feelings towards her is not very civilised, is it?"

"But I had my punishment this morning when I found you'd left, and I knew I was back to square one," was his grim rejoinder.

"Square one? What do you mean?"

"I don't think you ever realised what it meant to love you, and to find that you didn't love me enough to put up with the snags of the only life I could offer you at that time," he answered bitterly. "That it was my own fault for closing my eyes to your immaturity didn't make it any easier to get through the first two years after our separation. It's not a process I want to repeat. Until you arrived for the Christmas cruise, I was more or less back on an even keel. Now, after last night, I'm hooked again."

"It was you who made last night happen," she pointed out.

"I didn't think you would agree. If you hadn't, I shouldn't have forced the issue. Didn't you know that?"

Katy shook her head. "I know that men can and do enjoy sex without love. You'd already made it plain you hadn't any love left for me. Last night, when you were in my bed, you never said anything loving to me. I felt I meant nothing to you. I was just a woman . . . any woman."

He stared at her, the muscles of his jaw clenching and unclenching.

"The only woman who has ever meant

anything to me," he said, in a low, strained voice. "How could I tell you I loved you, thinking you meant to marry Dracoulis? Last night I came close to hating you for being prepared to meet my terms. I'd hoped you would refuse. I could understand your apparent eagerness to marry him — how many women wouldn't be eager? — but I thought you would jib at the condition I made. When you woke me up in the night, I damn nearly killed you for what you seemed to have become."

"It never even crossed your mind that it was a last-ditch bid to recapture what we'd once had?"

"Not until this morning when Dracoulis sent for me and told me he knew about us, and that you'd turned him down and were on a flight from Malaga. At first he made out he didn't know where you'd gone. Then I lost my temper, and he told me."

"Oh, Charles! You haven't wrecked your career?" she exclaimed in dismay, although her concern was mixed with a dart of new hope at what this seemed to imply.

"No, though I shouldn't have cared if I had. When I thought he'd let you go off without leaving any address, and it might take me months to trace you, it was to hell with my career. You were all that mattered to me then, and Dracoulis saw I meant business and told me what I wanted to know. I have to ring him tomorrow, to tell him if I've succeeded in making it up with you — though God knows I don't deserve to, after last night."

He reached out and drew her to him, and this time his hands were gentle on her slim shoulders. "Have I made you detest me?"

She shook her head. "Nothing you did to me could ever do that, Charles," she told him unsteadily.

He saw her lips quiver, and heard the break in her voice. Pulling her close, he pressed her head against his broad shoulder. "What a stubborn fool I've been not to see that now you're everything I wanted you to be from the beginning! Even then, if I'd been wiser, we could have weathered all those squalls. I asked too much of you, Katy . . . and gave too little in terms of patience and tolerance."

"No, no — it was all my fault. I wanted it all my own way, and it wasn't a way any worthwhile man could have tolerated." She raised her face and looked up at him. "Oh, Charles, tell me you still love me."

"I never stopped."

He bent his tall head and kissed her, gently at first and then with a swift resurgence of the passion of the night before.

She clung to him, hardly daring to believe that this wasn't a dream from which in a moment she would waken to find herself sleeping alone, doomed never again to feel his strong arms around her, except in the tormenting fantasies created by her subconscious mind.

For a long time they stood locked together until at last he picked her up, and asked huskily, "Where are you sleeping?"

This time he did not toss her roughly on to the bed, but lowered her gently and, seating himself beside her, took her hand and kissed it. "Oh, God, how I've missed you, Katy," he murmured, his lips in her palm.

She put up her free hand and drew his face down to hers.

When she woke it was daylight. She couldn't think where she was. But even before recollection of her surroundings returned to her, she was conscious of a golden feeling of happiness instead of the grey depression which had for so long hung like a low cloud over her spirit.

The door opened and Charles entered, carrying a tray.

"Ah, you're awake. I thought I might have to shake you. Every time I've looked in you've been sleeping like someone drugged," he said, as he set the tray down on a stool. "Do you want to brush your teeth before breakfasting?"

"Yes, please." She sat up and flung back the bedclothes. "What time is it?"

"Nearly noon."

As she sprang off the bed, intending to retrieve her nightdress which was lying on the carpet where he had tossed it nearly twelve hours ago, he intervened to kiss her good morning and, at the same time, to run his hands over the smoothness and warmth of her bare skin.

"Be quick." With a light slap on her bottom, he despatched her in the direction of the bathroom.

"How long have you been up?" she asked, when she rejoined him, clothed in a light cotton wrapper, her face washed and her hair brushed.

"Since about nine. Soon after I was up, Dracoulis rang. Do you want to get back into bed, or will you sit there?" — indicating a chair by the window. —

"There. He said he would ring when he called me last night to make sure I'd arrived safely. What did you tell him?"

"That I'd like a month's leave of absence for my second honeymoon. He told me I could have a fortnight."

"And then what?" she asked, remembering how adamantly Charles had dismissed her suggestion that she could live in his house at Fontainebleau between his leaves.

"It seems he does have it in mind to promote me when the Captain retires, and meanwhile he's prepared to stretch a point and allow you to live with me on board. I should have objected to that if he hadn't already explained the reason why he asked you to marry him. In the circumstances, I don't think living on board should cause you any embarrassment, although it will mean separation when we want to have children."

"They can wait for four or five years.

For the time being I only want you," she told him, as he handed her a glass of orange juice.

"And I you. We'll cross that bridge when we come to it. For the present I've made some arrangements which I hope will meet with your approval."

She smiled. "I should think they might. What are they?"

"I've hired a car in which we'll drive slowly south to rejoin *Artemis*. And I've booked a room at an hotel which I know is good for tonight. After that we'll rely on the Michelin guides. Nowhere is crowded at this time of year. This afternoon, on our way out of Paris, I thought you might like to have a quick look at my place at Fontainebleau."

"Oh, yes, I should like that very much."

So it was that, later in the day, having seen her eventual home which was very much as she had visualised it, Katy and Charles returned to the southbound side of the sweeping Autoroute du Sud which would take them another hundred kilometres before they turned off for the chateau, now an hotel, where they were to spend the first night of their leisurely journey.

Katy had always loved France more than any other country in Europe and, although in the northern part of it, the weather was chilly compared with that of southern Spain, the absence of sunlight did not trouble her.

Through the long years of their separation, even on the most beautiful days the climate in her heart had never been anything but wintry. Now, had they been driving through a blizzard, her mood would still have been springlike.

Much of the way she sat with her head slightly turned to the left in order to feast her eyes on the strong-featured profile of the man beside her; and from time to time he would glance briefly at her, with a warm, smiling look in his eyes which had never been there on board the yacht.

It was dark when they drove through the gateway and up the long tree-lined drive to the turreted mansion which might have been forty rather than only four kilometres from the great traffic artery between Paris and Marseille.

A log fire was blazing in the cavernous stone hearth of the vast, oak-beamed entrance hall. Katy watched her husband sign the register and felt a bridal stab of happiness at being, once again, Mrs Charles Ormond. The equality fanatics might not approve of a woman submerging her identity in that of her husband, but it gave her positive pleasure to travel under Charles's banner after four years of unwanted, unhappy independence.

Another fire was burning in their large bedroom, although the far side of the room by the two tall windows was equally warm because there was central heating as well as the cheerful, aromatic blaze of the pine logs.

Scarcely had their baggage porter departed before a waiter arrived, wheeling in a trolley of champagne in an ice bucket which Charles must have ordered when booking the room.

It was furnished with fine antique pieces which perhaps had been there before the chateau became an hotel. The bed was huge, fully eight feet wide, its gilded posts partially concealed by hangings of period needlework which had been relined with pale green silk to match the pleating on the underside of the canopy.

Katy was reminded of the dogaressa's

bed in the Owner's suite on board *Artemis*. Perhaps this bed, too, had been made in Italy long ago, and brought to France at the time when Catherine de' Medici had been Queen of France and introduced many enrichments to the culture of her country-by-marriage.

As she had when Andreas had shown her his famous bed, Katy looked at this bed and wondered about the men and women who had slept in it through the centuries, sometimes close to each other, sometimes as far apart as its spaciousness allowed. Many births and deaths must have taken place under its canopy, and undoubtedly many brides had, until very recent times, had their first lesson in love in it.

She was thinking that tonight she and Charles would join the long list of unknown lovers who had slept in it, happily entwined, when he introduced a prosaic note by coming to where she was standing, and saying, "Let's hope the mattress isn't a period piece."

But as he handed her a glass of champagne, the look in his eyes was at variance with his lighthearted remark. The renewed heat of his desire for her was almost as tangible as the warmth from the burning logs.

As he raised his glass in an unspoken toast to their shared future, she knew that, although some women might think her a fool for rejecting the opportunity to occupy the dogaressa's bed, and enjoy all the luxuries of being a millionaire's wife, for her the pleasures of wealth could never compensate for the absence of love. And that was something which only one man could give her; the man who was watching her over the rim of his glass and, with his other hand, drawing her gently towards him.

THE END

DEATH TRAIN
Robert Byrne

The tale of a freight train out of control and leaking a paralytic nerve gas that turns America's West into a scene of chemical catastrophe in which whole towns are rendered helpless.

THE ADVENTURE OF THE CHRISTMAS PUDDING
Agatha Christie

In the introduction to this short story collection the author wrote "This book of Christmas fare may be described as 'The Chef's Selection'. I am the Chef!"

RETURN TO BALANDRA
Grace Driver

Returning to her Caribbean island home, Suzanne looks forward to being with her parents again, but most of all she longs to see Wim van Branden, a coffee planter she has known all her life.

A GREAT DELIVERANCE
Elizabeth George

Into the web of old houses and secrets of Keldale Valley comes Scotland Yard Inspector Thomas Lynley and his assistant to solve a particularly savage murder.

'E' IS FOR EVIDENCE
Sue Grafton

Kinsey Millhone was bogged down on a warehouse fire claim. It came as something of a shock when she was accused of being on the take. She'd been set up. Now she had a new client — herself.

A FAMILY OUTING IN AFRICA
Charles Hampton and Janie Hampton

A tale of a young family's journey through Central Africa by bus, train, river boat, lorry, wooden bicycle and foot.

SEASONS OF MY LIFE
Hannah Hauxwell and Barry Cockcroft

The story of Hannah Hauxwell's struggle to survive on a desolate farm in the Yorkshire Dales with little money, no electricity and no running water.

TAKING OVER
Shirley Lowe and Angela Ince

A witty insight into what happens when women take over in the boardroom and their husbands take over chores, children and chickenpox.

AFTER MIDNIGHT STORIES,
The Fourth Book Of

A collection of sixteen of the best of today's ghost stories, all different in style and approach but all combining to give the reader that special midnight shiver.

FATAL RING OF LIGHT
Helen Eastwood

Katy's brother was supposed to have died in 1897 but a scrawled note in his handwriting showed July 1899. What had happened to him in those two years? Katy was determined to help him.

NIGHT ACTION
Alan Evans

Captain David Brent sails at dead of night to the German occupied Normandy town of St. Jean on a mission which will stretch loyalty and ingenuity to its limits, and beyond.

A MURDER TOO MANY
Elizabeth Ferrars

Many, including the murdered man's widow, believed the wrong man had been convicted. The further murder of a key witness in the earlier case convinced Basnett that the seemingly unrelated deaths were linked.

MORNING IS BREAKING
Lesley Denny

The growing frenzy of war catapults Diane Clements into a clandestine marriage and separation with a German refugee.

LAST BUS TO WOODSTOCK
Colin Dexter

A girl's body is discovered huddled in the courtyard of a Woodstock pub, and Detective Chief Inspector Morse and Sergeant Lewis are hunting a rapist and a murderer.

THE STUBBORN TIDE
Anne Durham

Everyone advised Carol not to grieve so excessively over her cousin's death. She might have followed their advice if the man she loved thought that way about her, but another girl came first in his affections.

BUTTERFLY MONTANE
Dorothy Cork

Parma had come to New Guinea to marry Alec Rivers, but she found him completely disinterested and that overbearing Pierce Adams getting entirely the wrong idea about her.

HONOURABLE FRIENDS
Janet Daley

Priscilla Burford is happily married when she meets Junior Environment Minister Alistair Thurston. Inevitably, sexual obsession and political necessity collide.

WANDERING MINSTRELS
Mary Delorme

Stella Wade's career as a concert pianist might have been ruined by the rudeness of a famous conductor, so it seemed to her agent and benefactor. Even Sir Nicholas fails to see the possibilities when John Tallis falls deeply in love with Stella.

THE LISTERDALE MYSTERY
Agatha Christie

Twelve short stories ranging from the light-hearted to the macabre, diverse mysteries ingeniously and plausibly contrived and convincingly unravelled.

TO BE LOVED
Lynne Collins

Andrew married the woman he had always loved despite the knowledge that Sarah married him for reasons of her own. So much heartache could have been avoided if only he had known how vital it was to be loved.

ACCUSED NURSE
Jane Converse

Paula found herself accused of a crime which could cost her her job, her nurse's reputation, and even the man she loved, **unless the truth came to light.**

TIGER TIGER
Frank Ryan

A young man involved in drugs is found murdered. This is the first event which will draw Detective Inspector Sandy Woodings into a whirlpool of murder and deceit.

CAROLINE MINUSCULE
Andrew Taylor

Caroline Minuscule, a medieval script, is the first clue to the whereabouts of a cache of diamonds. The search becomes a deadly kind of fairy story in which several murders have an other-worldly quality.

LONG CHAIN OF DEATH
Sarah Wolf

During the Second World War four American teenagers from the same town join the Army together. Forty-two years later, the son of one of the soldiers realises that someone is systematically wiping out the families of the four men.

THE TWILIGHT MAN
Frank Gruber

Jim Rand lives alone in the California desert awaiting death. Into his hermit existence comes a teenage girl who blows both his past and his brief future wide open.

DOG IN THE DARK
Gerald Hammond

Jim Cunningham breeds and trains gun dogs, and his antagonism towards the devotees of show spaniels earns him many enemies. So when one of them is found murdered, the police are on his doorstep within hours.

THE RED KNIGHT
Geoffrey Moxon

When he finds himself a pawn on the chessboard of international espionage with his family in constant danger, Guy Trent becomes embroiled in moves and countermoves which may mean life or death for Western scientists.

NURSE ALICE IN LOVE
Theresa Charles

Accepting the post of nurse to little Fernie Sherrod, Alice Everton could not guess at the romance, suspense and danger which lay ahead at the Sherrod's isolated estate.

POIROT INVESTIGATES
Agatha Christie

Two things bind these eleven stories together — the brilliance and uncanny skill of the diminutive Belgian detective, and the stupidity of his Watson-like partner, Captain Hastings.

LET LOOSE THE TIGERS
Josephine Cox

Queenie promised to find the long-lost son of the frail, elderly murderess, Hannah Jason. But her enquiries threatened to unlock the cage where crucial secrets had long been held captive.

CLOUD OVER MALVERTON
Nancy Buckingham

Dulcie soon realises that something is seriously wrong at Malverton, and when violence strikes she is horrified to find herself under suspicion of murder.

AFTER THOUGHTS
Max Bygraves

The Cockney entertainer tells stories of his East End childhood, of his RAF days, and his post-war showbusiness successes and friendships with fellow comedians.

MOONLIGHT AND MARCH ROSES
D. Y. Cameron

Lynn's search to trace a missing girl takes her to Spain, where she meets Clive Hendon. While untangling the situation, she untangles her emotions and decides on her own future.

THE WILDERNESS WALK
Sheila Bishop

Stifling unpleasant memories of a misbegotten romance in Cleave with Lord Francis Aubrey, Lavinia goes on holiday there with her sister. The two women are thrust into a romantic intrigue involving none other than Lord Francis.

THE RELUCTANT GUEST
Rosalind Brett

Ann Calvert went to spend a month on a South African farm with Theo Borland and his sister. They both proved to be different from her first idea of them, and there was Storr Peterson — the most disturbing man she had ever met.

ONE ENCHANTED SUMMER
Anne Tedlock Brooks

A tale of mystery and romance and a girl who found both during one enchanted summer.